"This is sexual harassment!"

"This is mutual attraction," Ben contradicted. "We both knew that from the moment we set eyes on each other."

"Your ego is unbelievable!" Rachel gasped. "I wouldn't have you if you came gift-wrapped."

"If you prefer, we'll keep our personal and professional relationship strictly separate. That's fine by me."

"We don't *have* a personal relationship," she felt impelled to point out.

"We will, Rachel...."

KIM LAWRENCE lives on a farm in rural Anglesey, Wales. She runs two miles daily and finds this an excellent opportunity to unwind and seek inspiration for her writing! It also helps her keep up with her husband, two active sons and the various stray animals which have adopted them. Always a fanatical consumer of fiction, she is now equally enthusiastic about writing. She loves a happy ending!

Kim Lawrence

THE SEDUCTION SCHEME

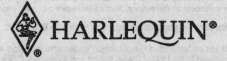

HARLEQUIN®

TORONTO • NEW YORK • LONDON
AMSTERDAM • PARIS • SYDNEY • HAMBURG
STOCKHOLM • ATHENS • TOKYO • MILAN • MADRID
PRAGUE • WARSAW • BUDAPEST • AUCKLAND

ISBN 0-373-12161-X

THE SEDUCTION SCHEME

First North American Publication 2001.

CHAPTER ONE

THE waiter lifted the lid of the silver tureen with a flourish. A closet romantic at heart, he gave a smile of satisfaction when the attractive young woman gasped in surprise.

Rachel was surprised. She'd known Nigel was going to propose tonight—he'd dropped enough hints—but she hadn't expected a gesture as theatrical and grand as this. Mouth slightly open, she stared at the diamond nestling on the velvet cushion as if it might leap out and bite her any minute.

Nigel Latimer leant forward eagerly in his seat; well satisfied with his companion's reaction, he nodded the waiter away with a conspiratorial grin.

'It doesn't bite,' he said, reaching over and taking hold of her hand. 'Try it on,' he urged. 'My God, Rachel, you're trembling.' Rachel, who was always so composed and in control. He was delighted and faintly surprised that his efforts had made such an impact.

Rachel tore her eyes from the sparkling ring to the spot where her hand was covered by a larger one. 'This is such a shock,' she lied shakily. It would offend him if she snatched her hand away, so being a considerate young woman she didn't.

Actually it had been obvious for weeks that this moment would arise; she'd thought about it a lot and now the moment was here she still didn't have the faintest idea what she was going to say! What a time to become indecisive.

She looked into Nigel's handsome, confident face, at his nice clean-cut features, the silvered hair that gave him the distinguished air that went down so well with his patients—

he looked every inch the successful, competent surgeon. Shouldn't it be excitement, not consternation that made her stomach muscles spasm? Some people didn't know when they had it good—and she, apparently, was one of them!

He expected her to say yes—and why shouldn't he? He was the answer to most women's prayers: good-looking, kind, wealthy. She sometimes wondered how a man like him had stayed single into his forties. Rachel found it unsettling when he called her the perfect woman he'd been waiting for all his life. His expectations of her were very high, so that she always felt almost as if she was playing a part for him. Perfect women always said the right thing at the right moment. How would he react if he discovered the less than perfect side to her nature?

He must love her to distraction to pursue her in the face of extreme provocation from Charlotte, her daughter. Did she love him? Did it matter? Weren't other things like companionship and compatibility more important? She was thirty now, past the age of expecting the fulfilment of adolescent fantasies.

The thoughts flickered through her mind in the blink of an eye. She felt a trickle of sweat slide down between her shoulder blades as she tried to respond the way she ought to. What's wrong with me? she asked herself. The first signs of concern were beginning to appear on Nigel's face when the waiter reappeared and apologetically announced that there was an urgent phone call for Miss French.

It wasn't just a desperate desire for a breathing space that made Rachel leap to her feet; the only person who knew she was here was the baby-sitter. What was Charlie up to now? she wondered in alarm.

She returned a few moments later and it was immediately obvious to her escort that all was not well.

'What's wrong, darling?' Nigel was at her side in a second. Rachel bit back a terrified sob. 'Charlie's disappeared!'

'There you are!' Benedict Arden flinched as a pair of small arms suddenly snaked around his leather-clad middle. 'See, I *told you* I wasn't alone.'

This last comment wasn't addressed to him but was thrown defiantly in the direction of a prosperous-looking middle-aged couple who were regarding him with dubious disapproval.

Having presented the sort of appearance for almost all the thirty-four years of his life that would dispose people like this couple to regard him in a benevolent light, Benedict permitted himself a small ironic smile at this fresh reminder of how important first impressions were before his thoughts returned to the more pressing issue: who the hell was this kid?

'This is your father?' Pity was mixed with scepticism in the woman's voice.

'Good God, no!' Revulsion flared in Benedict's voice as he took a step backwards.

He was relieved to find his wallet was where it ought to be, in the breast pocket of his leather jacket. The jacket was air force issue; he'd inherited it from his grandfather and it proved that he hadn't just inherited the face of a man he'd never known, but his build too.

The jacket combined with hair that had become long enough to be troublesome, plus a liberal sprinkling of dark stubble over his angular jawline, gave him an almost sinister aspect. At first glance, Benedict would be the first to admit, not the sort of character anyone would expect to find hugging a child, but then he wasn't doing the hugging.

The thin arms unwound and a pair of reproachful blue eyes looked up at him. Looking down into a delicate face, Benedict realised for the first time that the child was not, after all, a boy, but a girl—a girl dressed in androgynous jeans and

tee shirt. The realisation didn't soften his expression; the
menace that would have made sensible souls cross the road
didn't appear to make any impact on the child.

'He's my brother,' she continued, not taking her remark-
able china-blue eyes from his face. 'My stepbrother, actually;
my father married his mother,' she elaborated, warming to
the theme. A furrow developed between her brows as she
mentally composed a full family history. 'His father's dead
now.'

Benedict blinked as his parent was heartlessly disposed of.
This kid was unbelievable. You had to admire her sheer
cheek, even if she was mad or dangerous, or possibly a com-
bination of both! His lips quivered.

'It was probably the drink.' This, if recent comments had
been true, was the direction his son was driving him in—so
long as the vintage was good, of course. Nothing but the best
for Sir Stuart Arden.

He felt the swift exhalation of relief that made the child's
slight frame shudder and immediately regretted this frivolous
response as the blue eyes smiled approvingly up at him. He
wanted to groan; the last thing he wanted to do was encourage this lunatic child. As far as she was concerned he'd become some sort of co-conspirator. Like an idiot he'd let the
obvious opportunity to deny absolutely all knowledge of her
to pass him by. Well, he'd soon rectify that! He had plans.
He thought it unlikely that Sabrina had been pining away for
him, despite her assurances, and there had been a dearth of
single female company on the property his grandmother had
left him in the Australian outback.

'Do you think it's responsible to allow a child like this to
wander around the city at this time of night?' The woman's
lips pursed in distaste as she looked him up and down. The
man's expression showed no less disgust, but more caution.

He was also keeping a safe distance from the dangerous-looking character.

'No, I don't,' Benedict replied honestly. He could readily share this woman's sense of outrage. His eyes narrowed in anger as he thought of the irresponsible parents who robbed children like this one of their innocence by letting them roam the streets alone.

'Y-yes, well...' she stammered, thrown off her stride as much by the glint of anger in his dark eyes as his unexpected agreement.

'They tried to make me go with them, Steven.' The child had a very clear and penetrating voice. The male half of the couple looked embarrassed and alarmed as several people on the pavement, which seethed with a cross-section of humanity, glanced in their direction. 'Mum says I shouldn't talk to strangers!'

'We only wanted to take her to the police station.'

'Be my guest.' He felt dawning sympathy for this pair of Samaritans. He wanted nothing more than to hand the responsibility for this disreputable child back to someone who was obviously more qualified, not to mention more eager than himself. The joke had gone on long enough. As he took a step towards them the man backed hastily away.

'Well, all's well that ends well,' he said, taking his more reluctant wife's arm firmly. 'Goodnight.' The woman continued to cast suspicious glances over her shoulder as she was led away. Benedict watched their departure with dawning dismay.

'I thought they'd *never* go.' The skinny child abruptly released the hand she'd been holding. 'You were very useful.' She nodded towards him.

Benedict sighed; a conscience was a very uncomfortable thing to have sometimes. 'They were only trying to help. That's pretty commendable.'

'I don't need help.'

'The police station seems a good idea to me.' No matter how streetwise this kid seemed, he couldn't leave her to her own devices in an area that was crawling with undesirable persons. The child's next words made it obvious she considered him one of those undesirables.

'The police would have believed *them*.' She nodded in the direction where the couple had been swallowed up by the assorted bodies that thronged the pavement. '*You* don't look like the sort of person the police would believe at all. I picked you because you look scruffy and mean,' she told him frankly. 'I'd say you were trying to kidnap me and I'd scream very loudly. They'd believe me; that man thought you were going to hit him,' she ended triumphantly.

The kid's logic was flawless and her self-possession was staggering. A glance at his reflection in the plate-glass window told him she was right.

Recoil in horror had about summed up his mother's reaction to her younger son's appearance. His father had been less restrained. 'My God, he's gone native' and 'Get that bloody hair cut!' had been a selection of the more moderate pieces of advice he had offered. His teenage sister's response had been less predictable.

'You'll be mobbed by women who want to see if you're sensitive and misunderstood under the dark, dangerous exterior. Sexily sinister,' she'd said, quite pleased with her alliteration.

He'd found such perception in one of such tender years worrying; accustomed to female attention, he had already been aware of a subtle difference in that attention since he'd got back home—women were strange creatures. And talking about precocious—he had a more immediate problem than his hairstyle to worry about.

'If you don't want to go to the police station...' Maybe

this kid was already well known there, he surmised. He felt a stab of fury at the sheer injustice that any child's future could be so depressingly predictable. 'How about home?' He doubted home meant the same thing to this child as it did to him.

She still kept her distance, but his comment seemed to make her pause. 'The taxi driver said I didn't have enough money to go all the way home. I'll walk the rest of the way. I wanted to be back before...' The shrug was pure bravado. 'I'll be all right.' She bit her lip.

Despite the stoical exterior she couldn't keep the small tremor from her voice. It occurred to him that maybe she wasn't half as blasé as she pretended to be. The poor kid was probably scared stiff.

'I'll pay for your taxi.'

'You?' The young lips curled with scorn.

'You don't think I'm good for it?'

'I'm not about to get into a car with a stranger.'

'I'm pleased to hear it. I'm not going in your direction.' Walking through a minefield had to be easier than this!

'Why do you want to help me?'

Good question, Ben. This child certainly had an unnerving ability to cut to the heart of the matter. 'Such cynicism in one so young.' He suddenly remembered he was talking to a child. 'Cynicism is...' he began kindly.

'I know what cynicism is; I'm a kid, not an idiot.'

And that puts me in my place nicely, he thought, stifling an urge to smile in response to the youngster's scornful interruption. 'And I'm your guardian angel, so take my offer or leave it.' He made it sound as though he didn't give a damn.

'I think you're mad, but I do have a blister.' She looked down at her feet. 'New trainers,' she added, scuffing her toe on the ground.

*   *   *

'Follow that cab!'

The driver was quite happy to oblige once Benedict had paid up front. He'd be prepared to pay a lot more just to have the opportunity of telling that scrap's parents what he thought of them! Something about those eyes had made his protective instincts kick in with a vengeance.

The building the black cab drew up in front of was not in the sort of neighbourhood he'd expected. Rows of Edwardian villas lined the roads, and there was an air of quiet affluence. He watched as the kid walked up the driveway of a house as he got out of the cab.

She didn't see him until she had the key in the lock of the ground-floor flat. 'What are you doing here?'

'I'd like a word with your father.' Actually he'd quite like to throttle the irresponsible idiot.

'I don't have a father.' Her whole stance said, Want to make something of it?

'Well, your mother, then.'

'She's out. She won't be back until very late.' The door opened a crack and, slippery as an eel, she disappeared inside, closing the door behind her. 'Her boyfriend's going to propose to her tonight!' The last words were muffled as the door swung closed.

Images of a heartless, selfish woman so involved in her own pleasure that she neglected her child made his chest swell with righteous indignation. He'd heard definite tears in that tough little voice as the door had closed. Without actually thinking past his need to tell this woman exactly what he thought of her, he leant hard against the doorbell.

The baby-sitter had begun to scream again at the mention of the police.

'Police? Is that really necessary, Rachel?'

Rachel French rounded on her escort, her grey eyes smouldering with anger. 'Necessary! It's eleven-thirty at night, Nigel, and my ten-year-old daughter is not only not in bed, she is not in the flat, or the building. She could be anywhere!'

Actually, considering the discussion they'd had earlier in the day, Rachel had a pretty shrewd suspicion where her errant child was heading. This knowledge only increased the wholesale panic that threatened to reduce her to a gibbering wreck. Fear lodged like a physical presence in her chest; she could smell it and taste it. She glanced at the baby-sitter who had collapsed onto the sofa. She couldn't lose it now; one incoherent wreck was enough! Her fingernails gouged small half moons in the soft skin of her palms, but her expression stayed composed.

'It w-wasn't my fault!'

'I didn't say it was. Charlie is very...resourceful. Did you say something, Nigel?' she enquired icily as a disparaging sound emerged from his throat.

'Resourceful is one word for her; I could think of others...' He'd been goaded by the frustrating events of an evening which he had planned so meticulously into forgetting his usual tactful reticence.

'At another time I'd be only too delighted to hear your opinion...'

'Rachel, darling, I'm—'

'In the way,' she supplied, her urgency making her brutal as she shrugged off the unwanted protection of the arm he had draped across her shoulders. 'Susan, what time was it when you last actually saw Charlie? Not just heard the music in her bedroom, actually *saw* her. I know you're upset, but it's very important.' She stifled her natural impulse to wring the information out of the girl and forced herself to sound calm and reasonable. It took every ounce of her will-power. 'We need to know how long ago she left.'

'I...I'm not sure,' the girl sniffed. 'I was revising...the finals are next week.'

Rachel bit back the scathing retort that hovered on the tip of her tongue. To say her interest in this young woman's academic future was tepid would have been an exaggeration.

'You were being paid to look after the child, not study.' Nigel's accurate but ill-timed observation reduced the young woman to incoherent sobs once more.

'Nigel,' Rachel snapped, 'will you be quiet?' The loud and continuous sound of the doorbell interrupted her. 'Charlie!' she breathed, hope surging through her body.

'Will you stop that and go away?' The door opened a crack. 'I didn't want Susan to know I've been—'

'Charlie!'

'Mum!' The child released her hold on the door and Benedict took the opportunity to push it open. The source of the first cry stood at the other end of the hallway. A slim-fitting lavender-coloured floor-length gown was gathered in one hand, a mobile phone in the other. She let go of both; one slithered around her shapely calves and the other hit the big, distinguished-looking man with the silver-grey hair directly on the nose.

'I'll kill you, you little wretch,' the low, intriguingly husky voice that evoked a response like fingers gently moving up his spine announced lovingly.

Benedict didn't think this was likely, unless you could hug a person to death. The woman had dropped onto her knees and the child had walked straight into her arms.

'Are you all right? How *could* you?' Rachel was torn by equally strong desires to berate and kiss her daughter. 'Hush, it's all right now,' she murmured as the slender frame was shaken by silent sobs.

Rachel noticed the man standing behind her daughter for

the first time. How sad—the lights were on but there was definitely nobody home! It instantly struck her as tragic that someone so sinfully beautiful was lacking the intelligence to lighten those heavy-lidded, almost black eyes. She pressed her daughter's damp face into her bosom and looked briefly into the blank face. Jaw slack, eyes glazed and vacant, he stared back dully. Latin extract, she decided; there was nothing Anglo Saxon about his olive-toned skin and glossy black hair.

'Who's this, Charlie?'

'That's...Steven. He fetched me home. I thought I'd get back before you were home, Mum. How did you know...?'

'Susan rang us, of course.'

'Susan doesn't usually look in after John arrives. Just my luck!'

'*John?*' Rachel turned her attention to the baby-sitter who hovered nervously in the background.

'My boyfriend. He sometimes comes to keep me company. He had to go home early tonight.' Her tear-stained young face turned an unattractive shade of red as she studiously avoided Rachel's eyes.

'How fortunate for us he had a prior engagement.' Rachel pushed the wing of soft brown hair that had escaped her smooth chignon from her face and the sparkle of anger faded from her eyes. She could afford to be magnanimous now she had her daughter back. Her fingers slid down Charlie's silky, jaw-length blonde hair and she felt weak with relief. Things could have been so different.

Her eyes returned to the magnificent hunk in the doorway. A very unlikely Samaritan, she thought, gratitude misting her eyes.

Benedict hoped the groan was only inside the confines of his skull—*incredible* eyes! Pale skin that had an almost translucent quality and slightly slanted almond-shaped eyes that made the onlooker overlook the fact that her features weren't strictly symmetrical.

'I'm sorry, Miss French; it's just John and I don't get to see one another much. We've both got part-time jobs to supplement our grants and—'

Rachel's weary voice cut through the young woman's babble. 'I've no objections to you having your boyfriend's company, Susan. I just don't like you neglecting Charlie. It's been a long night. Perhaps you should be going home.'

'Right…sure, I'll get my things.'

She turned her attention back to her daughter, noting the sure signs of exhaustion in the delicate young face. 'Well, young lady, was it worth it?' The post-mortem and the chastisement would come later.

'You know where I went?'

'It didn't take a genius, love.' The argument they'd had over her standing with hordes of equally youthful, adoring fans in front of a theatre in the hope of catching a glimpse of her favourite boy band as they arrived at an awards ceremony had dragged on for two days. Charlie had capitulated rather too easily, which ought to have set the alarm bells ringing.

'Actually there was such a crowd, I couldn't see a thing,' Charlotte confessed. 'The taxi driver overcharged me and there were these nosy people…'

'Quite a little adventure,' Rachel murmured with great restraint. She knew it didn't do any good to dwell on what might have happened, but it was hard to control her wayward imagination.

'Is that all you're going to say?' Nigel asked incredulously.

Mother and daughter turned with identical frowns to look up at him. Although there was little physical similarity, at moments like this their relationship was very apparent. Rachel straightened up gracefully, her arms around her daughter's shoulders, the two of them unconsciously presenting a united front.

'At this precise moment, yes,' she said quietly.

'The child needs punishing; she needs to know what she did was wrong.'

'It's none of your business!' Charlie flared, pulling out of her mother's arms.

Rachel sighed. 'That's no way to speak to Nigel. He was very worried about you.'

'No, he wasn't! He doesn't even like me.'

Rachel winced as her daughter slammed the sitting-room door behind her. 'Sorry about that, Nigel.' She noted with dismay the pinched look around his nostrils.

Even though she knew Nigel's ill-judged comments stemmed from the best possible intentions, Rachel couldn't help but sympathise with her daughter's viewpoint. It had been just the two of them for so long, she couldn't help but resent his well-meaning efforts to share the burden of responsibility herself at times. Do I want to share the responsibility? a tiresome voice in her head piped up.

'Are you?' He ran a hand through his well-ordered hair and sighed. 'I'm sorry, Rachel,' he said stiffly. 'It's just tonight was meant to be special...'

'Well, we're not likely to forget it.' Her impish grin faded as there was no glimmer of answering humour in his handsome face. 'Perhaps we should just forget tonight ever happened.'

'Are you trying to tell me you *don't* want to marry me?' Incredulity filled his voice.

'Of course I'm not.' *Am I?* The thought filled her with guilt as she looked at the hurt expression on Nigel's face.

Her intention to kiss him, Rachel moved forward. She'd kicked off her high-heeled shoes earlier and the silky fabric of her long gown caught a loose nail in the skirting-board.

'Damn,' she muttered as the fabric snagged. 'Oh, thank you.' A large, capable-looking hand had freed the hem with surprising delicacy. Irrelevantly she noticed that despite his dishevelled appearance the shapely hands seemed very well cared for. As the young man straightened up his dark eyes looked directly into her face; the smile on her lips frayed ever so slightly around the edges.

She mentally binned her earlier label of simple but kind. There had been nothing simple or even particularly kind in the dark glance. Her stomach muscles quivered and she waited a little breathlessly for the sensation to stop. She'd never been this close to so much sheer *maleness* in her life. The distant noise in her ears sounded very similar to warning bells.

She was still grateful but her gratitude was now tempered with a degree of caution. There had been intelligence in those midnight-dark eyes and a confidence bordering on arrogance, a complacency common to all attractive male animals who knew they were the cream of the crop. It wasn't a confidence she associated with someone who worried about where his next meal was coming from.

Come to think of it, he didn't look undernourished—far from it. She felt an unexpected wave of heat under her skin as she assimilated his lean, muscular build and broad, powerful shoulders. It didn't matter what clothes he was wearing— he'd stand out in a crowd. Stand out in crowd nothing—the crowd would part to let him pass! He had an indefinable aura of someone who'd never been jostled in his life.

'I don't know how to thank you.' Angry that she could be distracted by anything as inconsequential as a well-developed thigh, she thought her voice came out crisply prim. *For heaven's sake, Rachel, this man has saved Charlie from God knows what and you're sounding snooty because he stands*

*out in a crowd? You can't hold the fact that he oozes sexual
magnetism against the man.*

What could she do to thank him? It was beneath him to
even think it, but Benedict couldn't stop mentally forming
the obvious trite response. At least he could think again, even
if the thoughts were too crass to share! He'd experienced lust
at first sight before, but never anything quite so mind-
numbing as those first few moments when he'd set eyes on
this woman—Rachel. He liked the name, he liked—

'For your trouble...'

Benedict stared at the notes in the boyfriend's outstretched
hand and his narrowed eyes moved slowly to the older man's
face. Forty if he was a day, he thought in surprise. What did
she see in him? Apart from the air of affluence, he thought
cynically.

'I don't want your money.' He didn't bother to disguise
his contempt.

Rachel elbowed Nigel in the ribs and glared at him as she
brushed past. 'Please don't be offended,' she said urgently.
'Nigel only meant—'

'Pay off the loser—he lowers the tone of the neighbourhood?'

'Now look here...' She wasn't surprised Nigel didn't
sound his usual confident self. That thin-lipped smile and
dark stare would dent anyone's assurance. Rachel doubted he
was accustomed to being regarded with such dismissive contempt.

'Nigel!' she remonstrated in a tone betraying more exasperation than sympathy. He was acting as if this were his
house, his daughter, his debt to repay. Couldn't he see he'd
trampled on the man's pride? Her tender heart was wrung
with empathy. 'Perhaps it would be better if we said goodnight now. Charlie—'

'Are you asking me to go? Fine...'

'Don't be silly, Nigel.' It was unfortunate he sounded like a sulky schoolboy.

'You're very considerate of *his* feelings.' This accusation took her breath away. 'What about me?' The childish whine was back. 'One of the things I like about you is your unemotional, level-headed attitude, Rachel, but just occasionally it would be nice to get a response that's not... Forget it!' he said, compressing his lips and throwing one last glance in the stranger's direction.

'I'll ring in the morning, Rachel, and don't forget we're dining with the Wilsons on Tuesday. Wear something a little less...' his eyes dwelt critically on the loose, soft, low cowl neckline of her dress '...revealing. You know how conservative Margaret is.'

The apology died dramatically on her lips as Nigel left. Usually she could ignore his comments about her clothes. They were normally couched in such subtle jocular terms that it wasn't possible to take offence, but this time it wasn't possible to disregard the criticism.

With a frown she peered downwards. The shoestring straps had made it impossible to wear a bra beneath the dress, but it wasn't as if she was displaying a vast expanse of cleavage—she didn't *have* a vast expanse of cleavage to display! Not that she was exactly flat-chested. She plucked at the folds of fabric and squinted down at the shadowy outline of her firm breasts.

'Oh, damn and blast it to hell!' she said defiantly, letting the fabric fall back into place. Trying to please Charlie, trying to please Nigel, she was tired of walking a damned tightrope. She was also pretty tired of feeling constantly guilty.

The faint indentation between her arched eyebrows deepened and her head fell back, revealing the graceful curve of her lovely throat. For a split second Benedict wondered what she'd do if he kissed her on that fascinating spot where the pulse visibly beat against her collarbone. Scream bloody murder, you fool, he told himself sternly, putting a lid quick smart on this foolish fantasy.

'Was that my fault?'

Her eyes flickered upwards and he could see she'd forgotten he was there. A flood of self-conscious colour washed over her pale skin. She glanced nervously down to check that the gown was covering what it ought and Benedict's lips twitched.

'No, of course not. I really am very grateful, you know, and I'd like to say thank you, without…'

'Bruising my feelings?' he suggested. His words brought a rueful smile to her lips and a twinkle to her eyes.

'How can…?'

'I missed my dinner bringing…Charlie home. A sandwich…?' He accompanied his words with a smile that had been melting female hearts since he was five years old.

Invite a man that looked like this into her home? Cautious instincts instilled from an early age fought a brief battle against her deep sense of maternal gratitude.

She gave an almost imperceptible nod. 'Follow me.'

He'd already proved himself trustworthy when he'd brought Charlie home. So he looked dangerous with his long hair and unshaven face, not to mention those sexy dark eyes, but all that was just superficial and she'd told Charlie often enough not to judge by appearances… All the same she couldn't dismiss the flutter of uncertainty in the pit of her belly. It did seem a lot like inviting the wolf into your house when you ought to be boarding up the door.

Charlie appeared as they entered the sitting room and Rachel's heart twisted as she saw how tired her daughter looked.

'Has he gone—?' She broke off when she saw the tall figure behind her mother. 'What are you doing here?' She sounded more curious than critical.

'Mr.... Steve is hungry.'

'So am I.'

'Bath and bed in that order.' To Ben's surprise, Charlie shrugged, grinned and obeyed the instruction. 'Have a seat,' Rachel then invited.

He did, and looked around with undisguised curiosity. 'Nice place.' If it was true that a room reflected the personality of the owner, Miss Rachel French's lovely exterior hid an uncluttered, unpretentious but warm interior. It was a lot easier to live with than the seventies retro look the designer he'd let loose on his own place had left him. He spread his long legs in front of him and gave a satisfied sigh. It was too late to go to Sabrina's now anyhow.

'Do you...do you have a place?' She removed her eyes self-consciously from the tears in his worn jeans. Her vivid imagination had conjured up some sordid squat.

He looked into her concerned grey eyes; she looked almost embarrassed. Obviously she thought he was comparing her good fortune to his lack of it.

'I have a place.' She looked relieved and he felt a bit of a rat, but not enough of a rat to come clean. 'Not as nice as this,' he said sincerely. If she knew his address she wouldn't believe his sincerity.

'I didn't meant to pry; it's just there's a lot of homelessness...'

'Are you a do-gooder, Rachel?'

She was instantly conscious of the casual way he used her name. He had a nice voice—deep and easy on the ears. Well, a bit more than easy on the ears, really, she admitted ruefully. It probably came in very useful in the seduction stakes.

'You make it sound like an insult. Some people do genuinely care, you know,' she said earnestly. 'I'm know I've been fortunate and I also know that pity isn't a very constructive emotion.'

'But it's a very natural one,' he said. Somewhere along the line the roles had got reversed. Wasn't she supposed to be putting him at ease?

'It's a bit late to be talking about social inequalities,' she said lightly. 'I'll make you that sandwich.' Suddenly she felt the need to escape those velvety brown eyes.

'Can I help?'

Rachel was alarmed that he'd followed her into the small galley kitchen. His presence made the small space seem even more confining. Whatever his domestic circumstances, there was nothing wrong with his personal hygiene; if there had been she'd have known it in the confines of the tiny room. He didn't ladle on the masculine fragrance with a heavy hand like Nigel, thank goodness! He smelt so male, she thought, breathing in appreciatively. Abruptly her spine stiffened. What am I doing? she thought in confusion.

'No, it's fine. Will cheese do? I don't have much; tomorrow's shopping day.' As if he was interested! She knew she was babbling and couldn't stop.

The chances were he was well accustomed to the effect he had on women—he probably traded on it. He knew his way around the female psyche all right, and probably the female anatomy too! She suddenly imagined the long, sensitive fingers that lay lightly on her work surface touching pale skin, and she shivered.

'Cheese will be fine. Charlie tells me you're getting married.' Elbows bent behind him, he leant back on the countertop.

Rachel bent down to retrieve the knife she'd dropped, the action hiding her flushed cheeks. Just how much had her daughter confided to this stranger? she wondered in alarm. Her alarm was given an extra edge because she realised that the skin she'd been visualising his hands touching was her own! Lack of food was obviously affecting her brain! She pushed a slice of cheese into her mouth and hoped this would give her flagging blood sugar a boost.

'Children don't miss much,' he said with the comforting certainty of someone who knew about these things. Actually he didn't know much about children; his sister would be insulted to be included in that category and his niece was a baby of seventeen months whom he'd not seen above twice in her young lifetime. 'And I couldn't help but overhear...'

'Charlie doesn't miss much.' Rachel dropped the knife in the sink and pulled a clean one from the drawer. 'She's very bright—with an IQ that makes me feel inadequate sometimes. It's easy to forget how young she is on occasion.' She had begun to wonder whether it had been a good move coming to the city to be close to the school that specialised in 'gifted children'; Charlie didn't seem to be settling in at all.

'And are you?' Getting married, that is?' he added.

'I don't know.' Now why the hell did I tell him that? she wondered. Perhaps it was just a relief to speak to someone who didn't have a vested interest.

'It must be hard bringing up a child alone,' he mused casually. 'I suppose it would be a relief to find someone to share the responsibility with, especially if he's loaded...'

'I'm not looking for a father for Charlie. Or a meal ticket.' She felt her defensive hackles rising. Was he trying to get a rise, she wondered suspiciously, or was he just plain rude?

'Just as well—the father bit, I mean.' She gasped audibly and he smiled apologetically into her face over which a definite chill was settling. 'The cosy rapport was noticeable by its absence. She seems to hate his guts.'

Rachel found herself responding with a rueful smile even though she felt vaguely uneasy at the intimacy developing in this conversation with a total stranger.

'Charlie has very definite views,' she admitted. 'But, as much as I love my daughter, I don't let her vet the men I see.' *'Men'* made her social life sound a lot more interesting than it was. Over the past ten years how many had there been? No calculator required, she thought wryly. 'Mayonnaise?'

'Yes, please.'

'Help yourself,' she said, sliding the plate in his direction.

'Thanks.' Benedict pulled out one of the two high stools that were pushed underneath the counter. 'Aren't you eating?' Two stools, he noticed, not three; boyfriend didn't stay over too often, then. He felt a surge of satisfaction.

Rachel thought of the meal she'd never got to eat. 'I lost my appetite somewhere between losing my child and fighting with my fiancée.'

She glanced down at her finger and realised she'd never actually picked up the ring. She'd never actually said yes. She didn't believe in fate, but it did seem as if someone was trying to tell her something. Perhaps there was enough of the romantic left in her to wish she could marry someone she genuinely didn't want to live without. Someone whose touch she craved. A man with whom she could share her deepest dreams and fears—who would make her feel complete.

'Do you do that much?'

For a horrified split second she thought she'd spoken out loud. It took her another couple of confusion-filled seconds to realise he wasn't referring to her fantasising and then make the connection with her earlier comment.

'I don't make a habit of losing Charlie.' What a night; it's no wonder my concentration is shot to hell, she thought.

'I meant fighting with your boyfriend—though he's hardly a boy, is he?' He took another healthy bite of the sandwich and watched the angry colour mount her smooth cheeks. He'd touched a nerve.

'Nigel is forty-two,' she snapped back, her fingers drumming against the work surface. 'I've not the faintest idea why I'm justifying myself to you!' she muttered half to herself.

'Don't worry…'

'I wasn't!'

'You probably feel uncomfortable about the age gap.'

'Age gap!' she yelped. This man was stretching her maternal gratitude to its limit. 'I'm thirty.'

'Really? You don't look it.' Time might blur the edges of her beauty in the distant future, but with a bone structure like that the ageing process would be graceful.

The dark, direct stare was deeply disturbing. 'Am I supposed to be flattered?' she asked sharply to hide the fact that this unkempt man was making her feel flustered and more self-conscious than she could recall feeling in years!

'I can do better than that…'

'I'm sure you can.'

'But I wouldn't presume.'

Her brows drew together in a straight line as she looked at him. 'I find that difficult to believe.' He had the look of a man who'd do a lot of presuming.

'Has he ever been married?'

'As a matter of fact, no. And he's *not* gay!'

'I'm sure you did the right thing asking.'

'I didn't ask! Nigel is a cautious man, and he's seen lots of his friends' marriages break up.' She didn't add that Nigel had always seemed more appalled by the financial havoc this wrought when he'd mentioned the marital failures of his peers. 'There's nothing wrong with caution.' She winced at the defensive note in her voice. There wasn't a single reason why she needed to justify herself to this man.

'Not a thing. Not unless it makes you deaf to gut instinct.'

'Nigel isn't too big on gut instinct,' she said drily. She bit her lip, immediately feeling disloyal for voicing this opinion.

'And you?'

'*Pardon?*' The icy note in her voice didn't alert him to the fact that he was being unacceptably personal. Wasn't that just typical? Just when you needed them, the tried and tested remedies let you down...

'I suppose there are times when a lady like you just can't afford to listen to her gut instincts,' he reflected slowly. She searched his face suspiciously; she was certain, despite the gravity of his expression, she was being mocked. 'I mean, you couldn't just date any guy who wandered in off the street.' This time there was no mistaking his reference. 'Do you have a list? Suitable professions, salary, that sort of thing?'

'If you want to say I'm a snob...'

'I'm not really sure what you are,' he confessed. 'I'm feeling my way.'

'I don't want to be *felt*!'

'That explains Nigel's frustrated expression.'

'If you've finished eating...?' she said pointedly. She could see from his expression she was wasting her breath. Her haughtiness was passing right over his dark head.

'Has it always been just the two of you?'

'Are you always this curious about strangers?'

'Charlie made me feel like one of the family.' The flash of laughter in his eyes was reflected by the lopsided smile that tugged at one corner of his mouth. He didn't let her into the private joke.

'Really?' Her arched eyebrows shot up. 'That's not something she makes a habit of.'

'It's like that sometimes, don't you find? You meet someone and it feels as if you've known them for ever. You just click.'

His voice had a tactile quality when he lowered it to that soft, intimate level; it was almost as if he'd touched her—stroked her. She pushed aside this disturbing notion briskly, because the idea of being touched by this man was *extremely* disturbing!

'I try not to make snap decisions.' Panic was developing into an uncomfortable constriction in her throat. 'I'm sure you do a lot more...clicking than me,' she said tartly.

It occurred to her belatedly that it might be a mistake to swap sexual innuendo with someone she wanted to keep at a safe distance. She didn't want to give the wrong impression.

A laugh was wrenched from his throat. 'That sounded a lot like a snap judgement to me.'

'I didn't mean...' she began, horrified. She stopped; that was *exactly* what she'd meant. He had the look of a man who put his charismatic personality to good use with the opposite sex. A sensible woman naturally distrusted a man with such raw, in-your-face sexuality.

'Many a sexual athlete lurks behind horn-rimmed specs and a geeky exterior,' he warned, amusement in his face. 'So is it my social standing or physical appearance which places me in the no-go zone?'

He'd dropped the veiled pretence that this conversation was impersonal. Usually someone who welcomed straight speaking, she felt light-headed with an adrenalin rush that made her want to lock herself safely behind a closed door.

'I don't enjoy this sort of conversation.'

'No, I don't recall having a conversation precisely like this one before.'

'Mum, I'm ready.'

Rachel turned, an expression of false vivacity on her face. For once Charlie's timing was immaculate.

'Right,' she said briskly. Love swelled in her chest as she looked at the small figure. How could you feel cross with a child who looked at you with eyes like Charlie's? she wondered. Especially when those eyes were underlined by dark rings of exhaustion. 'You'd better say thank you to Mr...'

'Steve will do just fine.' A man called Steve wasn't born with a silver spoon firmly pushed down his throat...a man named Steve didn't choke on family obligations. He held out his hand and the sleeve of his jacket fell back to reveal the face of his Rolex. Casually he shook his cuff down. A pair of bright blue eyes followed his action.

'Thank you...Steve?' Small, delicate fingers were laid in his own; the guileless glance was knowing and slightly smug.

'I'll just see Charlie to bed for the *second* time tonight.'

Benedict watched them go, his expression thoughtful. Charlie didn't miss much at all, he mused.

Rachel had half expected her guest would be difficult to get rid of. She'd been rehearsing tactful ways to make him leave in her head. She felt vaguely deflated, and relieved of course—yes, she *was* relieved—to find him standing in the sitting room obviously waiting to go when she re-emerged from Charlie's bedroom.

'Thanks for the sandwich.'

'You didn't tell me where you found Charlie or how...' He hadn't actually told her much at all. She'd done all the revealing.

'You could say she found me,' he said. The statement made him grin for some reason.

'I'll never forget what you did.'

'But you'll forget me?'

She decided to ignore this challenge. Kissing him would be open to misinterpretation so she clasped one of his hands firmly between both of hers.

'I can't tell you how relieved I was to hear that doorbell. I've no doubt you think I'm the world's worst mother.' He was looking at her hands with a peculiar expression so self-consciously she let his hand go.

'For about two seconds, but first impressions can be misleading.'

She misunderstood the significance of his words. 'I expect you get a lot of that. I mean looking the way you do…' She closed her eyes and drew a deep breath. When you've dug a hole, Rachel, stop before it's too deep to climb out of, she told herself. 'There's nothing wrong with the way you look.' She couldn't resist trying to repair the damage.

'And there's nothing wrong with the way you look, no matter what the boyfriend says.' There was amusement rather than offence in his deep warm voice. 'A man who tells you what to wear will likely tell you what to think if you give him the chance. Goodnight, Rachel.'

'I won't let anyone do that.'

'Good girl.' He took her chin in his hand and placed his warm lips over hers. If this chaste salute was meant to keep her wanting more, it worked! The sensual impact left her body so taut and strung out, she might well have responded like some sex-starved idiot if he'd touched her again. He didn't.

'I won't say goodbye. I think we'll meet again very soon.'

Rachel watched him go with a dazed expression. She knew they were just words, but it didn't stop her wondering just what she'd do if he turned up on her doorstep one day.

CHAPTER TWO

'OH, WELL, if she's on loan from Albert at least she'll be easy on the eye.' Benedict's mouth twisted into a dissatisfied grimace. He wasn't happy at the idea of working with a stranger; Maggie's anticipation of his needs bordered on the psychic. 'All the same, Mags, I think it's pretty mean of you to desert me on my first day back.'

'I could stay to hold your hand if your sojourn down under has turned you soft. I don't understand a word of German, but I could look intelligent.' His secretary cast him an unsympathetic glance as she continued to flick through a file. 'Here it is! I don't know how it got there!' she exclaimed, retrieving a sheaf of papers. 'I want to leave everything as it should be for Rachel.'

The reminder of a familiar name brought a reminiscent smile to his lips. 'Would you really do that for me—cancel your holiday?'

'No, I can't wait to kick off the dust of this place,' came the frank rejoinder.

'So nice to see someone who enjoys her work.'

'Huh! Listen to who's talking. I didn't see you hurrying back. Besides—' the fashionable specs were pushed firmly up her retroussé nose '—I'm a legal secretary, not a slave—subtle difference, I know, but...'

Benedict sat down on the edge of his desk. 'PA sounds much more dynamic.'

'I'm not feeling too dynamic right now.'

'You'd *really* prefer to lie on a tropical beach with your husband than stay here?' he said incredulously.

'Call me peculiar... Ah, is that you, Rachel? Come along in!' she yelled as she heard a sound in the adjoining room. 'Rachel French, this is Benedict Arden. You probably haven't met; I think he was on walkabout when you started.'

Disbelief froze the polite smile on Rachel's lips. The possibility that she'd met a *doppelgänger* or long-lost identical twin was speedily dismissed—*it was him.*

Rachel wasn't sure how long the shock lasted or when it became full-blown fury. A wave of humiliation fanned the flames of her anger. Her thoughts all ended in a big question mark. Sick joke...? Well, whatever it had been she'd certainly been sucked in.

'Well, I'll leave you two to it. I've already shown Rachel the layout and I've warned her you'll work her to a shadow of her former self, and unlike me Rachel needs all the pounds she's got! So be nice to her.' She glared at her employer, affection thinly concealed beneath the spiky exterior.

'I will, Mags.' This could work out quite beautifully—then again maybe not, he thought, meeting the frozen hostility of his new assistant's eyes.

'He works so hard himself he doesn't realise the rest of us have a social life.'

Maggie hadn't noticed anything, Rachel realised incredulously. She maintained her tight-lipped silence; if she said what she wanted to she just might lose her job! Screaming abuse at the big boss's son had a habit of doing that. *Social life?* The way she'd heard it Benedict Arden, son of Sir Stuart Arden, the head of Chambers, managed a very creditable social life. The sort of social life beloved of society pages. What the grapevine hadn't told her was that he got his kicks from humiliating those on a less elevated social plane.

Whilst her features remained immobile her scorn spilled out into the grey of her clear eyes as they flickered briefly in his direction. That suit probably cost more than two months of her salary. In her head she'd furnished his home with rising damp and peeling paintwork—when she thought of the anxiety and guilt she'd felt when she'd pictured him in those surroundings! Her hands unconsciously balled into two fists. She was only vaguely conscious above the buzzing in her ears of Maggie's departure.

'So you work for Albert.'

'I do.'

'His secretaries always do have excellent...office skills.'

He wasn't looking at her office skills. 'Are you implying I got my job on the merits of my legs?' It was pretty hard to miss the fact that his eyes were on her legs, their slender length disguised by tailored fine black wool trousers.

'Don't get defensive. I don't think you're sleeping with the boss. Everyone knows Albert only ever looks; he's a happily married man.'

'That's a weight off my mind; I wouldn't want you to get the wrong end of the stick.' That was it, after this dignified silence, she promised herself.

'I expect you're wondering...'

'Not at all. Maggie has brought me up to speed. I've already provided translations of all the relevant documents. I don't know if you've had an opportunity to read them yet...?' she said briskly.

The heavy lids had drooped slightly over the alert dark eyes and he levered his long frame from the edge of the desk, straightening his spine. He was one of the few men she'd ever seen who could get away with long hair past their teens and he was further past his teens than she'd imagined. But why should this surprise her when nothing else she'd imagined about him had been accurate?

The newly shorn hair combined with the clean-shaven look revealed a deeply tanned, blemishless skin stretched tightly over a stunning bone structure. Fate and generous genes had

arranged all those strong planes and hollows in exactly the
right places, giving him a masculine beauty that was in no
way soft or pretty.

'We've got to work together...'

'Maybe.' She made it sound as though she had some
choice in the matter, which they both knew wasn't the case.
'I'll reserve my judgement on that. You do *look* the part.'
The way he looked was the way hungry young executives
all over the city dreamed about looking—from his highly
polished handmade shoes to his tasteful silk tie. 'But then
you're good at that...'

Why did I say that? she groaned inwardly. Anyone would
think I want to get the sack! A mental picture of all the bills
she needed to pay before the end of the month flashed before
her eyes. Be cool, professional, she told herself; he's not
worth the energy of losing your temper.

'So possibly we should clear the air?' he continued, as if
her acid observation had remained where it ought to—in the
privacy of her mind.

Rachel discovered resentfully that an eloquent quirk of one
dark brow could make her feel childish and petulant. 'I'm a
secretary; I don't require explanations, just instructions.'
Pragmatism lost out to the sort of antipathy that made her
skin sprout invisible thorns.

'Fine,' he said, some of the lazy tolerance evaporating
from his deep voice. 'Instruction one, sit down!' He grasped
the back of one pale wooden Italian-designed chair and
dragged it across the carpet.

'How dare you speak to me like that?' she gasped.

'*Please*,' he said, with a smile that made her realise the
guise she'd last seen him in had only revealed a danger that
was already in the man—disguised now by perfect tailoring
and a cultured air, but it was there all the same...bone-deep.

'That's better,' he approved as she reluctantly sat down in the chair he'd indicated.

His fingers brushed against the back of her neck as he released his grip on the chair and she tried not to react. She prayed the sensation that crawled over her skin was revulsion—anything else she couldn't cope with!

'Why are you angry?'

She automatically twisted her head to look at him—was he being serious? 'I'm not.'

'Surprise,' he continued as though she hadn't spoken, 'amazement, curiosity... I experienced those when you walked through the door. I can identify with the gobsmacked state—'

'You didn't look very gobsmacked to me.'

'I hide my emotions behind a suave exterior,' he said blandly.

'Are you laughing at me?' This very definite suspicion only increased her deep sense of misuse.

'Why the anger, Miss Rachel French? And don't bother denying it; your eyes have been flashing fire since you first saw me.'

To hell with office politics—she was going to tell him what she thought of him: walking into her life and disappearing just as abruptly, leaving a vague sense of dissatisfaction and restlessness in his wake...

'I *hate* frauds.' To think he'd infiltrated her thoughts enough to make her wonder, at the most unexpected moments, what he was doing. Now it turned out his lifestyle was indeed far removed from her own, but not in the direction she'd imagined! She doubted he wanted rescuing from his pampered, privileged existence.

'I didn't lie precisely.' A quick mental review confirmed this was correct. His ethics weren't so irreproachable that he wouldn't have bent the truth a little if required.

'Steven…?'

'That was Charlie's idea.'

'Why would my daughter make up your name?' she said scornfully.

'It had something to do with claiming me as her long-lost brother. I took to it right off; there's something solid and dependable about a Steven. Admittedly I'm not Steven, but I'm still the man who rescued your daughter—despite her opposition, I might add.'

He had to remind her, didn't he? Rachel chewed her full lower lip distractedly; she couldn't deny the truth of his observation—at least the bit she could follow. The part about brothers made no sense at all.

'You were laughing at me—us. I'm sure you'll dine out for the next month on the story: "what happened when I went slumming". I felt *sorry* for you!' She couldn't have sounded shrill if she'd tried but indignation did make her rather deep, husky voice rise an octave.

'Pity is a very negative emotion,' he reminded her. 'Sorry, photographic memory. Only pity's not all you felt.' The way his dark eyes moved over her face alarmed her almost as much as the soft accusation. To her relief he didn't pursue it. 'I find it curious that you approved of me more when you thought I was one of the great unwashed. An unforgivable sin, I know, to turn out to be neither a paid-up member of the underworld nor a thug with a heart of gold. Has it occurred to you that your craving for a bit of…how can I put this delicately?…rough—' an inarticulate squeak of outrage escaped Rachel's pale lips and he reacted as if she'd uttered soothing words of encouragement '—could be a reaction against the sort of man you date? You're looking for someone outrageous and slightly dangerous.'

'I'm not looking full stop!'

'When I meet a woman she generally knows what I do,

who my family is and can usually hazard a fairly accurate guess at my bank balance...'

Rachel watched as he straddled a chair that was twin to the one she was sat upon. 'My heart bleeds...and you just desperately want someone to love you for the *real* you.' Her voice fairly dripped with sarcasm. 'Which is no doubt why you roam the streets looking like a drug dealer!'

'Do you make a habit of inviting drug dealers into your home?' he enquired with interest.

The fingers that were laid lightly along the back of the chair were very long and elegant, she noticed irrelevantly, and his hands were shapely and strong. His words made her hospitality suddenly seem worryingly reckless.

'I was grateful—' she began defensively, before his urbane, polished tones interrupted her.

'Was?'

'Am—I *am* grateful,' she said from between clenched teeth, sounding anything but. 'I was sorry for you if you must know.' That will teach me to get all sloppy and sentimental, she thought.

'You shouldn't blame yourself, you know. Your body is chemically programmed to find a mate. Hormones aren't too concerned with financial prospects or social standing.'

'Leave my hormones out of this!' she yelled.

'Fine,' he said, with a languid smile that made her want to scream. 'I can work with pity. As ulterior motives go, I think I prefer pity to avarice.'

'Only someone from an obscenely privileged background could say anything so stupid.'

'You have strong opinions about wealth, Rachel?'

'No, just you. I think you're a spoilt...irresponsible—' She broke off, biting down hard on her lower lip to stop further imprudent remarks escaping.

'I sense you were just warming to your theme,' he said,

with a provoking smile. 'Don't let the fact I'm your boss cramp your style.'

'Temporary boss.'

'Thank God, she breathed fervently?' he surmised.

'You're very intuitive.'

'And you're very suspicious, Miss French. Let's get a few things straight. When I met your daughter she was about to be carted off to the police station by a concerned couple. Being a child with limitless resources and a cool head, she decided to claim me as her brother. Apparently I looked mean enough to lack credibility in the eyes of the law *and* to get rid of the nice people—'

Rachel's angry glare turned slowly thoughtful. That *did* sound awfully like something Charlie would do. 'That doesn't explain the way you looked or the fact you made me think...' She shook her head doubtfully. 'Why didn't you just tell me?'

'If you work here you'll know I've just come back from a six-month stint on a cattle ranch in Queensland, and that's the only reason I lacked a certain sartorial elegance. The conclusions about my background were all yours and your charming companion's. How was dinner at the Wilsons'? Did you wear something suitable?'

Rachel stiffened, warm colour seeping under her skin. 'Nigel has a cold; we didn't go,' she ground out.

'I put Charlie in a taxi and followed her with the express intention of giving her delinquent parents a piece of my mind. It took me about ten seconds to realise I'd misread the situation, and less than that to be rendered speechless by your beauty...'

Rachel gritted her teeth and opened her mouth to tell him in no uncertain terms that the only desire such ridiculous statements evoked in her was one to throw up! Suddenly she recalled that vacant expression that had first made her think he was a bit challenged in the intellectual department. He couldn't actually be telling the truth—*could he*? For some reason this absurd notion impaired her ability to think straight.

'Don't say things like that!'

'This is the new me, open and transparent.'

'I'm not beautiful, I'm passably attractive.' Letting him see she was rattled seemed a bad idea. It wasn't too difficult to see how he'd achieved his reputation as a womaniser.

'As they say,' he remarked with an almost offhand shrug, 'it's all in the eye of the beholder, and this beholder,' he said, touching his chest with an open hand, 'sees beauty. I also see a kind heart.'

'A fact you ruthlessly exploited,' she reminded him, trying hard to cling to her sense of outrage.

'I was tempted,' he admitted, 'but I didn't think your charity would extend as far as a bed for the night.'

She gave a gasp of outrage. 'You were right!' Had he *no* shame?

'I feel much better now we've sorted that out,' he confessed with a sigh. 'I was wondering how I was going to bite the bullet and tell you I'm actually quite respectable. I was hoping my disreputable appearance didn't account for all of the attraction, and if you have a thing about leather...'

'*Respectable!*' she choked incredulously. 'Am I supposed to believe you'd ever have remembered me except as an amusing story to relate over dinner?'

'Oh, believe it,' he said, placing his chin in one cupped hand that rested on the chair-back. Suddenly he wasn't laughing at all. Rachel thought the expression in his eyes should have carried a government health warning; happily she was immune to shallow flattery. She could be objective about the ripple of movement in her belly and the rash of gooseflesh that erupted over her hot skin.

'It also makes it all much simpler to ask you out to dinner,' he added cheerfully.

'I'll speak slowly and clearly because I can now see my first impression of you was correct...'

'What was your first impression?'

'Muscularly overdeveloped and intellectually undeveloped—a beautiful imbecile!' she flared in a goaded voice. She realised too late the revealing nature of this confession. 'I have a fiancé,' she hurried on swiftly. 'I don't date other men.'

'I don't see a ring,' he remarked sceptically.

'We have an understanding.'

'He didn't seem to understand you too well the other night. Nice bloke, no doubt, but a bit lacking in the imagination department.'

Of all the arrogant, *impossible*... 'For your information Nigel is *very* imaginative,' she spat back.

'I'm happy for you,' he said solemnly. Confused, Rachel stared back. 'A good sex life *is* important.'

'I didn't mean Nigel is imaginative in bed!' She hated knowing he'd made her flush to the roots of her hair.

'I didn't really think he was,' Benedict responded, nodding sympathetically.

The blood was pounding in her ears. 'Nigel is worth ten of you!'

'That's being a bit severe,' he remonstrated. 'I did detect the very early stages of a paunch, but that's to be expected in men of a certain age. He seemed very well preserved to me. Tell me, are your parents still alive?'

This apparently inexplicable change of subject tipped the balance away from inarticulate fury and towards confusion. 'No, they're not; my aunt Janet brought me up.' Janet French had been there all her life and the recent loss of the lady with the indomitable spirit still hurt badly.

'An all-female household,' he said triumphantly. 'I thought so, and now there's just you and Charlie. You're looking for a father substitute, not a lover, Rachel.'

'Lame-brained psycho-babble.' Her lip curled with genuine scorn. 'This is sexual harassment.'

'This is mutual attraction; we both knew that from the moment we set eyes on each other. If I wasn't a gentleman I'd have done more than kiss you goodnight. Only I wanted to know if the attraction wasn't totally the forbidden fruit thing. I see now it isn't.'

'Your ego is unbelievable!' she gasped. 'I wouldn't have you if you came gift-wrapped.'

'Is that a fetishist thing? he enquired. 'Because I have to tell you I'm not really into that sort of thing.'

'And I'm not into smutty innuendo!'

'If you prefer, we'll keep our personal and professional relationship strictly separate. That's fine by me. A freak set of coincidences is the only reason this conversation is taking place in the work environment. We needed to clear the air.'

And he thought the atmosphere was clear! The only thing that was clear to her was that she ought to keep her dealings with Benedict Arden to a minimum.

'We don't have a personal relationship,' she felt impelled to point out.

He was persistent; you had to give him that. If her circum stances had been different she might even have been flattered. Be honest, Rachel, he *is* extraordinarily attractive, she told herself.

If she'd been a carefree, single thirty-year-old, who knew? Temptation might have overcome good sense. But she wasn't. She had a child, responsibilities. She didn't act on impulse—she *couldn't* act on impulse. She'd done that once when she was a naive nineteen-year-old and she knew all about consequences—not that she'd ever regretted the decision to keep her child.

'We will, Rachel,' he said with an unshakeable confidence she found disturbing.

'I'm a single mother.'

'So? I'm not applying for the post of father. Do you only date potential daddy figures, Rachel? Had you decided what you were going to do when Steve knocked on your door?'

The sly question slid neatly under her guard. 'You! Given a choice, I wouldn't have you within a fifty-mile radius of my daughter!' His words had held an edge of mockery that made her long to hit him. What did Benedict Arden, the self-confessed hedonist, know about bringing up a child alone?

'You know something? You're even more shallow and two-dimensional than office gossip has led me to believe. It may shock you but it's not all that unusual for people to consider someone else's feelings other than their own.'

'You want to know what I think?' He remained palpably unmoved by her passionate annihilation of his character.

'Would it make any difference if I said no?'

'I think you'd decided to open the door to Steve, and not just to prove you're not a snob.'

Rachel fixed a scornful expression on her face, though she knew his words would return to haunt her when she was alone later. Steve hadn't existed but this man did and he had all the same bold sexuality. She instinctively knew that Benedict Arden was the more dangerous of the two.

'You're flesh and blood, not a machine; you can't control your feelings. You're a single woman who happens to have a child. You're never going to marry good old Nigel, because when it comes right down to it, despite all his admirable qualities, he bores you rigid.' He nodded with satisfaction as a revealingly guilty expression crept across her features. 'I'm not asking you to do anything that will emotionally scar your daughter, I'm asking you to break bread with me and possibly open a bottle of wine—even two if you're feeling reckless.'

'Do you always do *exactly* what you want?' she asked resentfully.

An odd expression flickered across his face, deepening the lines around his mouth and bringing an inexplicable bleakness to his eyes. 'I'm here, aren't I?' he said cryptically. He pulled at the silk tie neatly knotted around his neck as if the constriction suddenly bothered him. 'Are you free tonight?'

'I don't even like you.' His mercurial temperament made it hard to keep up with his chain of thought.

'Liking will come—I'm a very likeable guy; ask anyone.' His smile held an attractive degree of self-mockery. 'We could settle for mutual attraction for starters. Think about it,' he advised. He glanced at the Rolex on his wrist. 'The meeting with Kurt is in twenty minutes—right?'

Rachel glanced at her own watch and realised with a sense of shock that she'd forgotten completely about the morning's tight schedule.

'Yes,' she said uncertainly.

'When I had dealings with him last year he brought his own translator; you must have made an impression. You're fluent in German?' He stood up and Rachel followed suit. The switch into impersonal mode had been subtle but distinct.

'German, Italian and French,' she confirmed. When the translator hadn't turned up she'd enjoyed the opportunity to utilise her skills.

She ought to have felt happy now they were on ground she felt confident about; she knew she was good at her job. Albert had taken over a portion of Benedict's work, which was mainly corporate law, whilst he'd been out of the country, but this particular client had worked with Benedict before and wanted him to take charge now he was back in harness. She'd had the impression that Albert had been more than happy to relinquish the complicated case.

The client also wanted her, so she'd been transferred too to stand in for Benedict Arden's PA who was taking annual leave. At the time she'd been quite happy to agree. At the time she hadn't known who Benedict Arden was.

'Why aren't you working as a translator?'

'I did when Charlie was a baby—manuscripts mostly.'

'From home?' She nodded. 'That must have been quite an isolating experience.'

His perception startled her. 'When childcare became easier I worked for a law firm near home.'

'Where's home?'

'Shropshire.'

She paused, realising with a sense of shock how adept he was at drawing out information without revealing anything himself. Or maybe not—the memory of that bitter expression in his eyes when he'd implied he would have preferred not to be here flickered into her mind. She wondered whether she'd interpreted his economic words correctly. Was he already disillusioned with his career or did it simply interfere with his taste for the high life?

'That's where the aunt brought you up. And would I be way off the mark if I suggested this aunt wasn't too keen on men?'

'Experience taught me to be cautious, not indoctrination.'

'Charlie's father?'

'My daughter is not a subject I discuss with strangers.'

'You're the subject I'm interested in, but if it makes you feel happier I'll put that on hold.'

It didn't make her feel happier but she welcomed the breathing space. She soon learnt, as she worked in close contact with him throughout the day, that, though she might doubt his dedication, his competence was undeniable. He caught on fast and had a knack of homing in on small but significant details that would take most people hours of arduous toil to discover. There had been none of the languid playboy about the man she'd worked with today, and despite herself she found the seeds of admiration germinating.

'We work well together, don't you think?' She slid the last file into its place and didn't respond even though she was overwhelmingly conscious of his presence. 'Don't tell Mags I said that; she'll think I'm being disloyal. What time shall I pick you up?'

'Pick me up?' She couldn't delay looking up; there was nothing left to fuss about with on her neat desk—where was an errant paper clip when she needed it?

'For dinner.'

'It's a girls' night in with a pizza take-away, and even if it wasn't I don't want to go out with you.'

'Staying in would suit me.'

'I'm trying to be polite.'

'Don't worry about manners; you should have left half an hour ago. This is your own time—be as rude as you like,' he said generously.

'Why are you doing this?'

He seemed to consider the question seriously and she had the fleeting impression that he was almost as puzzled as she was. 'Hormones?'

It wasn't the reply she'd expected and she almost laughed out loud. That might be construed as encouragement, however, so she carefully wiped all trace of amusement from her face.

'Are you just not used to being knocked back? Is that what this is about? Are you one of those men who's more interested in a difficult chase? You lose interest once you've caught your prey?'

'In answer to your first question I've had my fair share of rejection…'

'Sure…' she drawled.

'Your disbelief is very flattering.'

'It wasn't meant to be.' Her aching jaw told her she was grating her teeth again.

'I'd enjoy accepting your surrender as much as you'd enjoy offering it.' The heat coursed through her body so unexpectedly, the breath was trapped in her suddenly tight chest. She was angry with herself for allowing the sudden mental image of 'surrender' to throw her into such total confusion.

'But all that stuff about the chase being more fun is pure junk. As to the endurance of these feelings, who can ever tell how long that will last?'

Surrender! Was she really some sort of pathetic creature who fantasised about surrendering to male dominance?

'Give me strength.' The ring of defiance she heard in her own voice was deeply disturbing. 'Are we talking hours or days here?' she hurried on, wanting to erase the sound of her own lack of conviction.

'Does durability lend respectability to sex? I can guarantee quality, not—'

'Staying power?' she suggested, sliding her arm into the tailored jacket that matched her trousers.

'Here, let me.' She either had to comply or indulge in an undignified scuffle so she willed herself to accept his help passively.

'Can't I tempt you?'

There was the faintest tremor in her fingers as she fumbled over the buttons of her jacket. Benedict remained standing behind her, his hands still at either side of her shoulders. Despite the gap of air that separated them she could almost feel the imprint of his fingers; it was quite a bizarre sensation.

Was this the same sort of phantom pain amputees suffered? What a ridiculous analogy, she told herself, irritated by the whimsical idea; he's not part of my body. *He could be.* Shock at the mental picture that accompanied this maverick thought made her suck in air through her flared nostrils and extinguished the dreamy, unfocused expression in her eyes.

Even as she turned to look at him and firmly shake her head in refusal, the honest answer to his question was ringing in her mind. Not only could he tempt her, *he did.* Even though she knew he was shallow, deceitful, self-indulgent and definitely not for the likes of her, she actually wanted—no, *wanted* didn't begin to cover the craving that had taken over her body. Her treacherous hormones had conspired against her.

As devastating as this sudden self-awareness was, she was determined to keep it in proportion and not be overwhelmed—she *could* cope. Her intellect and emotions weren't involved; she could rise above what amounted to basic lust.

'Tell Charlie that Steve sends his love,' Benedict called after his secretary.

It looked to him as though she was about to break all records for escaping from the building. Or was it just him she was trying to escape? Whistling softly to himself as he pondered this question, he walked back into the inner office.

CHAPTER THREE

'WHERE are you off to?'

Rachel registered that the solid object she had walked into was the chest of her temporary boss. 'S-sorry,' she gasped. So much for the cool, professional distance she'd vowed to keep. After a single morning of detachment she was flinging herself into his arms.

She was seized by a sudden strong and bizarre urge to blurt out her troubles. This is the wrong person and wrong place to indulge in an orgy of shared burdens, Rachel, she told herself firmly as she attempted unsuccessfully to pull clear of the protective circle of his arms. She'd learnt to handle life's crises alone some time ago.

'Is it the appeal of sandwiches in the park? I'd join you myself if I hadn't already promised to lunch with the revered parent.' The quizzical, teasing expression left his face as he took in her pale features. 'What's wrong, what's happened?' he demanded, taking her by the shoulders. The smell of the soft, lightly floral perfume she used tantalised his nostrils. That haunted expression in her wide eyes was doing the strangest things to him.

'I'm sorry but I have to go... Charlie...it's an emergency. I left you a note... I have to go.'

Hands flat against his chest, she tried to push past. God, what must he think of her? Only their second day working together and she was running off. She didn't care what he thought of her; there was such a thing as priorities. He'd have to wait for explanations.

'Hold on, what's wrong?'

'I know it's not convenient, but I—'

'Forget about what's convenient and tell me what's wrong.'

'The headmistress rang; Charlie's at the casualty department...'

She didn't get any further. 'Which hospital?' He nodded when she told him. 'Come on, I'll take you.'

'What...?' On the very few occasions when her meticulous childcare arrangements had not stretched to cover a domestic disaster that required her presence, at best her previous bosses had displayed impatience; at worst they'd been openly critical of her lack of professionalism.

'I thought you were in a hurry.'

'I am.' A sudden smile of pure relief spread across her face. The journey by underground and taxi would have taken her over an hour, with every second an agony of anticipation. 'I can't impose,' she began doubtfully.

'Shut up, Rachel; I'm trying to show you what a nice guy I am. Don't spoil it. A lift should be good for at least a dinner date.' His mouth curved in a lopsided smile and when she looked half suspiciously into them his eyes were kind and concerned, not predatory.

'On me,' she promised fervently.

Seeing the glow of gratitude in her marvellous eyes, Benedict decided he might just have undervalued his services. She didn't object to the light touch of his guiding hand on her shoulder as they left the building.

He racked his brains to recall one instance when he'd actually put himself out to please one of his lady friends and failed, but then the disasters in his previous lady friends' lives had tended to lean in the direction of broken nails or an inability to get a hair appointment, not hospitalised children!

Rachel pulled aside the cubicle curtain to reveal a pathetic sight.

'Oh, *Charlie*!'

'I know I look terrible, but the hair will grow back; they had to shave off the little bits to stitch up the cuts. The blood's from my nose.' She touched the gory front of her once pristine school shirt. 'I'm not cut anywhere and I didn't break anything.'

'Congratulations,' Rachel said drily as she sat down on the edge of the trolley.

'They want to throw me out so I must be fit.'

'And does Mrs Faulkner want to throw you out too?' When Rachel had left the headmistress in the reception area with Benedict the lady had looked almost as stressed as she felt.

'I hope so. It's a crummy school. They all think they're so smart.'

'And you don't?' Charlie's new punk-spiky hair made her look incredibly young.

'That's different,' she said impatiently.

'But *fighting*, Charlie?'

The thin shoulders hunched defensively. 'He was much bigger than me; I wouldn't hit a little kid. And I didn't hurt him; I fell down the steps before I had the chance to,' she admitted honestly.

'Mrs French?' The nurse stepped into the room. 'If she gets any of the symptoms on this card—' Rachel skimmed anxiously over the card which was pushed into her hand '—bring her back. Ten days for the sutures. Your GP will remove them; here's a letter for him. Sorry to rush you but we're busy this afternoon.'

She'd whipped the paper sheet off the trolley which Charlie had just vacated and disappeared before Rachel could mumble her thanks.

The headmistress was deep in conversation with Benedict when they returned to the reception area; she looked almost animated as she listened to what he was saying and a lot more relaxed. For once Rachel had reason to be grateful for his effortless charm; she needed the head mistress as softened up as possible. This was one tête-à-tête she wasn't looking forward to.

'Miss French, perhaps we could have a word?' Her eyes slid to Charlie. *'Alone?'*

'I know you don't get into cars with strangers, Charlie, but with your mother's permission perhaps you'd like to look over mine,' Benedict said.

'What do you drive?'

'A Mercedes.'

'What sort?'

He told her, and her eyes widened in admiration.

'Wow!' She looked hopefully in her mother's direction.

When Rachel returned to Benedict's car a few minutes later her daughter was deep in what appeared to be a technical discussion with Benedict.

'Sorry to keep you waiting,' she said, looking through the open window of the passenger seat.

'I wasn't bored,' Charlie said happily. 'He doesn't know *anything* about this car,' she informed her embarrassed mother.

'I do now,' Benedict said drily.

'I was apologising to Mr Arden, not you, Charlie. We'll get a taxi home of course.'

'Don't be stupid, Rachel.' Before Rachel had an opportunity to complain at this form of address she was distracted.

'Rachel!'

She spun around, startled at the sound of a familiar voice. 'Nigel!' she said, staring at him in blank amazement. 'What are you doing here?'

'I work here, remember? More to the point, what are *you* doing here?' His expression changed as he recognised the small, spiky-headed figure in the front seat of the car. 'Charlie's been in the wars, I see. Why didn't you ring me, darling?'

So that was why the name of the hospital had sounded so familiar. The sound of the endearment made her feel oddly embarrassed.

'It was all such a rush. I got a phone call at work and Mr Arden kindly offered me a lift. How are you feeling? Is the cold better?' How could she admit she hadn't even thought about Nigel? She'd forgotten he even worked in the hospital!

'I'm fine...fine,' he said hurriedly. 'That was kind of Mr Arden. Have me met?' he asked, looking directly at Benedict, a puzzled frown pleating his brow.

Rachel held her breath.

'It's possible,' Benedict admitted calmly. 'Ben Arden's the name.'

'Any relation to Sir Stuart Arden?'

'My father.'

'I can see the resemblance.' Benedict nodded neutrally; he knew he was a genetic throwback to his Italian maternal grandfather and bore no resemblance to his very Anglo-Saxon-looking parent. 'We're in the same golf club,' Nigel explained affably.

Rachel could see the umbrella of social acceptability obviously extended to Sir Stuart's offspring.

'Give me a minute, Rachel, and I'll take you home.' He reached in the breast pocket of his white coat to retrieve his urgently buzzing pager.

'Don't worry yourself; it's on my way,' Benedict assured him.

Rachel met Benedict's benign smile with a look of seething frustration. Now that the immediate panic was over the last thing in the world she wanted was to get in that car with him.

'That's very good of you,' Nigel responded, with a grateful smile. 'I'll ring you tonight, Rachel.'

Whilst she was receiving a peck on the cheek—Nigel wasn't the most tactile person in the world—she was overwhelmingly aware of the brown eyes watching her every move. This awareness probably had something to do with the fact that she turned her head and kissed a somewhat surprised Nigel full on the lips.

He looked bemused but pleased, and Rachel immediately felt guilty for using him. She was going to have to put a stop to this—she should have already. The knowledge weighed on her conscience like a stone.

'Slide into the back, Charlie, and let your mum sit up front.'

Rachel saw that Nigel looked a bit startled when the child immediately did as she was bid. 'Maybe a knock on the head wasn't such a bad thing,' he joked softly to Rachel as she slipped reluctantly into the soft cream leather upholstery beside Benedict. Nigel waved them off cheerfully.

'What did he say to make you look so murderous?' Benedict asked curiously as they pulled away.

'It was nothing,' she said shortly, avoiding his probing eyes. She told herself she was being over-sensitive—Nigel had only been joking. She knew she shouldn't compare Benedict's light touch with her daughter to Nigel's heavy-handed approach, but it was hard not to contrast their very different styles.

'I prefer Steve. *Benedict.*' Charlie screwed up her small nose, her expression speaking volumes.

'My friends call me Ben if that's any help.'

'Ben.' She tried it out experimentally. 'Not bad,' she conceded. 'I thought it was cool when Mum said she was working for you.'

'Mr Arden to you,' Rachel put in sharply. Trust Charlie to

take a shine to him; that was *all* she needed. Where was that well-known disagreeable personality when she needed it?

'Mum was really mad when she found out you'd fooled us,' Charlie piped up from the back. 'I don't think she's forgiven you yet.'

'Is that so?'

'Take a nap, Charlie; you look tired,' Rachel observed hopefully. She knew from experience that short of gagging her child there wasn't much chance of stemming the flow of indiscreet comments.

'I wasn't worried about you, like Mum.'

'You weren't?'

'No. I saw the real expensive watch you were wearing so I knew either you were a good thief or an eccentric rich guy.' With a satisfied smile she settled into her seat.

'You worried about me?' Rachel could hear the slightly smug smile in his deep, expressive voice. Why did this man's voice have the same effect on her as half a bottle of red wine? she wondered resentfully. It did have a marvellous texture; she found herself whimsically likening his warm, rich tones to being wrapped up in a rich, luxurious velvet sheet and pulled herself up short. The less she thought about sheets and Benedict Arden in the same context the better!

'No more than I do any other destitute social outcast,' she observed with a dispassion she was far from feeling.

She'd never admit it was the man more than his condition that had got under her skin, but fantasising about someone she'd never meet again had seemed a fairly harmless thing to do. There was safety in distance and she found herself wishing she had more than a couple of feet to protect her right now.

They continued to travel in silence for several minutes. In the back Charlie fell asleep. When she noticed this Rachel worriedly fished the card the hospital had given her out of her bag and scanned it.

'"Sleepy or difficult to rouse".' She read the words out loud and glanced anxiously at her sleeping daughter. 'Do you think...?'

'She's just asleep, that's all, Rachel. She's had quite a day.'

Strange how a second opinion made things slip back into perspective. Rachel's smile was strained; she took a deep breath and tried to calm down. She tried really hard not to be a fussy, over-protective mother, but sometimes...

'I expect you think I'm just a neurotic mum.'

'I think you've perfected the mum part, Rachel, but I think you've neglected the woman part.'

His words startled her and made her feel uneasy. 'You're saying I'm not feminine.'

'You're about the most feminine female I've ever met.'
Her stomach went into its now familiar acrobatic contortions as his dark eyes moved warmly over her face and lower... Give me strength—*please*, she prayed without much confidence that anyone was listening. In the wider view her libido probably came pretty low down priority-wise.

'You're just overcompensating for being a single parent. When did you last do something for yourself?'

'What do you mean?'

'I mean something spontaneous, selfish...'

'I'm not a spontaneous sort of person.'

'You must have been once.' She saw his eyes touch the image of her sleeping daughter in his rear-view mirror and her expression grew chilly.

'I don't think that's any of your business.'

'Granted,' he acknowledged easily. He changed tack. 'How do you think Charlie will feel if in eight years' time she realises that you've built your whole life around her needs?'

'I haven't, I don't!' she protested angrily. He knew nothing about her—nothing! She recalled uneasily that Aunt Janet—more tactfully, of course—had insinuated something similar last year.

'It's highly likely she'll feel guilty when she wants to be independent and go her own way. You're not doing her any favours by living your life vicariously through her.'

'I don't!'

'Not yet, but you have definite leanings in that direction.'

'You know nothing about being a parent.'

'Perhaps an impartial critic is what you need.' It occurred to him that the impartial bit was getting less accurate by the minute.

'Charlie will *always* be the most important person in my life,' she breathed passionately.

He nodded slowly as if he understood her passion. His next words took her totally by surprise.

'Have you *got* a life, Rachel?'

'I used to think so until you turned up and with a few words of worldly wisdom showed me the error of my ways.' She shot an acid look at his perfect profile. '*You* telling me *how* to live! If it wasn't so ridiculous it would be laughable. You don't live on the same planet as the rest of us; you're just a pampered—'

'I realise a few distinguished grey hairs and a nice line in pomposity would lend me more credibility on the advice front...'

The dig made her jaw tighten. 'Am I supposed to believe all this interest and concern is totally altruistic?'

He flicked an almost amused look at her heated face as he pulled up in front of her flat. 'I never imagined you were naive enough to think that,' he observed with provocative gravity. 'Why do you get so aggravated when I'm nice to you, Rachel? Are you by any chance afraid of liking me?'

It was so obvious she couldn't understand why she hadn't figured it out for herself. Afraid? She was petrified! He wouldn't intend to destroy her life but then she didn't imagine tornadoes had inherently evil intentions either.

Benedict was the sort of man people loved—she mentally sidestepped the chasm that opened up at her feet. The sort of man who would leave a great gaping hole when he moved on. Already Charlie liked him, and she was an intense little creature who didn't let people close often—but when she did... No, it was totally irresponsible to let a man without staying power into her life. He hadn't even attempted to disguise the fact that his intentions were of the dishonourable kind.

She laughed, achieving a brittle sort of condescension that she was proud of. 'You're so charming...' Hand on the door, she swivelled slightly in her seat to look at him.

There was a movement behind the liquid darkness of his eyes that said even more clearly than the febrile contortions of the erratic muscle beside his mouth that she'd succeeded in aggravating him. She hadn't wanted him to like it, had she? So what was the problem?

'Perhaps you could let me practise it on you.'

Oh, help! What sort of can of worms had she opened now? That would teach her to be smart. Getting out of the car was definitely the right thing to do. If only her legs had been in full working order. If only he weren't looking at her in that wolfish way.

'You could give me a few tips on how to bring my performance up to scratch. It would be a generous gesture.'

'Ben...'

'Progress! She's said my name.' His gesture was too expansive for the confines of the car and his fingertips collided with the luxuriously upholstered roof. 'It wasn't so difficult, was it? Now, about my lessons...'

'You're b-being foolish,' she stammered, unable to tear her hypnotised eyes from his face. 'Charlie...' She wielded her daughter's presence as a last line of defence.

'Is sleeping like a baby.' His right hand was on the angle of her jaw; his thumb moved over her cheek, tracing the sweeping curve of one high cheekbone. Abruptly his expression intensified and grew into something breathlessly intimate—she was certainly pretty breathless, anyhow, and his breathing had noticeably picked up tempo!

'I really want to kiss you, Rachel French. Tell me you've thought about it too.' The muscles in the strong column of his neck worked hard as he swallowed.

Her own throat ached with emotion. 'It's safer to leave it there—in your mind,' she said huskily. A small corner of her brain informed her disapprovingly that she'd just made a confession.

The lethargy that had invaded her body screamed a different message entirely from the one she spoke. He had altogether the most fascinating mouth she'd ever seen. What would it feel like? Her mouth grew dry as she waited in breathless anticipation to have her question answered.

'Safer but frustrating.'

The sexy rasp of his voice made her tremble harder. This had to stop. 'Oh, for heaven's sake!' she snapped as the sexual tension reached breaking point. 'Get it over with.' She closed her eyes and leant forward.

There was a second's startled silence and then, to her amazement and chagrin, she heard the sound of his laughter; it began somewhere in the depths of his chest and emerged deep and uninhibited.

'My God,' he gasped, leaning back in his seat and wiping his eyes. 'You really know how to break a mood, Rachel.

You looked like a sacrificial virgin in one of those cheap B horror movies.' He started to laugh again.

Eyes fully open, she glared at him. 'I'm not a virgin.'

'I'd guessed that,' he confirmed gravely, the laughter now confined to his dark eyes. Eyes that had been smouldering seconds earlier.

To say she felt piqued was an understatement. Ridicule, rejection... He was heartless and insensitive to boot! So her technique had been lacking in a certain amount of finesse. She'd wanted him to...she still did, she acknowledged angrily. Well, if he wouldn't kiss her she'd just have to...

Half kneeling as she leaned towards him, she took his face between her two hands. Breath coming fast and hard, she deliberately covered his mouth with her own. Benedict froze, and as his lips remained passive and unresponsive under her own Rachel realised the enormity of the mistake she'd just made. Lips still pressed to his, her eyes opened.

She met his startled gaze and wanted to die of sheer humiliation. Even as she began to pull back the expression in the dark, hooded eyes changed. Seeing the change was like watching spontaneous combustion.

'Don't!' She felt the harsh command against her lips. Even had she felt the inclination, the strong arms that had moved across her back prevented her from withdrawing.

Eyes still holding hers, the pressure of his lips slowly parted hers. Suddenly a whole mindless, exciting world was within her grasp. Very slowly his tongue traced the silky outline of her lips. When her tongue darted out to meet his tentatively she could see the flash of sultry approval in his eyes. She was close enough to see the gold tips of his extravagantly long lashes and the fine lines around his eyes which would one day become permanent. Permanent and Ben weren't compatible terms.

The silky thrust of his tongue wrenched a deep groan from

her as it penetrated deep within her mouth. His dark features swam out of focus and her eyes closed.

Her arms wrapped themselves around his neck as if it was the most natural thing in the world. For several mindless, frantic moments they explored hungrily with lips, tongues and hands. She could hear the gasps and weak, bleating moans but didn't actually associate them with herself.

Though she'd managed to plaster herself very firmly against his impressive upper torso, it didn't feel nearly close enough to satisfy the fire in her blood. Her fingers pressed deeply into the sculpted outline of his broad back as she squirmed sinuously in his arms.

'Rachel…?'

She lifted her lips from the side of his neck and looked in a dazed fashion into his face.

'I think Charlie's waking up,' he said thickly.

Remembering who she was and where she was was a painful business. Horrified, she looked into the back seat where her daughter was stretching sleepily.

'Are we home?'

'Yes. How are you feeling?' Well, I've really done well on the keep-my-distance campaign, haven't I? she mocked herself inwardly. She couldn't even claim the excuse of moonlight and a romantic location. It was broad daylight and she'd been behaving like… She felt the skin of her neck burn as she remembered exactly how she'd been behaving. And *she'd* started it!

'I feel sore.'

'Where?' Benedict asked.

Charlie stretched and considered the question. 'Everywhere.'

Apprehensively Rachel stole a furtive glance in Benedict's direction. The smug satisfaction she'd half expected was absent; he looked… Distracted was as good a word as any to

describe his expression. As she watched he inhaled deeply
and ran a hand roughly through his hair. Recalling that she
was responsible for the ruffled condition of the short, sleek
style brought a fresh wave of mortification.

'Are you all right?'

'I'm falling apart at the seams' probably wasn't the response he was expecting so she smiled politely if distantly.
Now I'm distant, she thought wryly.

'You must be in a hurry to get back to the office.'

'Anxious to get rid of me, are you?'

'I wouldn't be so rude.'

'The impeccably mannered Miss French,' he drawled
slowly. 'I think you'd be quite a lot of things that would
surprise both of us—given favourable conditions.'

This thinly veiled reference to her recent wanton behaviour
was enough to send her almost tumbling from the car in her
anxiety to escape. He was almost as fast as her and much
better co-ordinated; by the time she'd opened the rear door
to help Charlie out, he had already scooped the uncharacter-
istically passive child into his arms.

'Lead the way,' he said cheerfully. Charlie giggled as he
swung her around.

'You'll make her throw up.' Rachel pursed her lips and
refused to enter into the spirit of things.

She didn't like being manipulated and she fumed quietly
whilst she did as he requested—at least it had sounded like
a request, but she knew an order when she heard one, no
matter how sneakily it was dressed up.

She was doing it again—letting him into her home—and
this time she knew exactly how dangerous he was! If she'd
been the sort of young woman to indulge in misty optimism
Rachel might have told herself that nothing had changed, but
she had a much more realistic approach to life. She knew
that walking away from that short burst of beautiful hormonal

insanity back there would require good judgement and careful handling. She was pretty sure she wasn't capable of either just now.

'Make yourself at home, won't you?' she said sweetly as, much to her annoyance, he placed Charlie at one end of the sofa and claimed the other end for himself. For once Charlie seemed prepared to tolerate adult foolishness as he tickled her feet which lay in his lap.

'Sure I'm not intruding?'

'Would it make much difference if I said yes?' What did a few kisses mean to him? A great big nothing—the answer was depressingly obvious.

He strolled into the kitchen a few seconds later and spoilt her efforts to regain her serenity. 'Charlie sent me to say she would like a milkshake, preferably chocolate.'

'I'm not at all sure I should reward her after what she's done.' She continued to clatter around.

'What are you doing?'

'Making a cup of tea.'

'Looks to me like you're just rearranging the cups.'

'I don't recall inviting you into my kitchen. It's too small and you're...you're too...too big,' she ended feebly.

What was she supposed to say? Having you this close is driving me to distraction? All I can think about is the way you tasted, the way you felt...?

'I'm a genetic throwback to my grandfather,' he explained apologetically. 'He was Australian, of Italian extraction—a big man by all accounts. My sister's the same, but Tom, my big brother, never made it past five ten. I think it's the scent that's heightened in an enclosed space.' The words emerged suddenly and his eyes widened with shock as though he was as surprised as she was to hear them.

'What?'

He wasn't looking at her; his eyes were fixed grimly on

his own hands, and that muscle beside his mouth had begun to throb again. 'Even after you've left a room it lingers, but in an enclosed space like this—or the car—it drives me crazy. It's so distinctive—not the pretty flowery stuff but that warm female smell that comes off your body.' His words emerged in uneven staccato bursts and his fingers, as they gripped the stem of a glass he'd idly picked off the draining-board, were white. Suddenly the stem cracked with a noise like a pistol shot.

'Sorry.'

'You're bleeding,' she said hoarsely as she watched the scarlet drops land on the white counter. He was watching the flow of blood with a peculiar lack of interest. 'Here, put it under the cold water.' She grabbed his wrist and thrust his hand under the tap.

'Florence Nightingale.'

'I could hardly watch you bleed to death in my kitchen,' she said gruffly. His forearm was covered in fine dark hairs; they felt surprisingly soft under her fingers. Stroking couldn't be designated as first aid, she told herself firmly, stifling some very strong urges in that direction.

'It's only a scratch.'

'That's very brave and macho of you, but it looks pretty deep to me,' she said worriedly. 'I've got a first-aid kit in the bathroom; don't go away.'

'It's good to be wanted.'

Wanted? If he knew the half of it…! Then again she'd not been exactly subtle so he probably did. As she rushed through the living room Charlie was engrossed in her favourite video. She ought to be concentrating on sorting out the latest disaster in her child's life—*fighting*, for heaven's sake! Instead what was she doing? Mooning over some beautiful body dangerously attached to a cunning mind.

She'd never be able to pick up her perfume without being

reminded of his words—words that had filled her with a savage exhilaration: he was hurting as much as she was. There was another, less palatable and unflattering explanation—he might just be recycling old and well-tried lines. He'd had so many women it wasn't reasonable to expect originality.

All the same he'd have to be a *very* good actor to fake that raw need in his voice. The downy hair over her body stood on end as she relived those breathless few seconds.

'Sorry if that hurts,' she said a few moments later as she applied pressure to the dressing to stem the flow of blood.

'It takes my mind off the other pain.'

'Which...?' She raised her eyes to his face and immediately wished she hadn't.

'I think you know what pain I'm talking about.'

She did now: his eyes were very eloquent. 'I won't offer you the use of my cold shower; I'm sure you've got a perfectly good one at home.'

'You'd consign me to seventies retro? Black tiles and mirrors on the ceiling? Cruel, cruel woman.'

'If you don't like it...' she began curiously.

'When asked my opinion I made the major error of admitting I didn't give a damn.'

'Why would you do anything so stupid?' She finished securing the light dressing with tape and stood back to observe her handiwork.

'Because I didn't care.'

'What a peculiar attitude.'

'You've done this before,' he said, turning over his bandaged hand.

'You've met Charlie—are you surprised? Though she's never gone in for fighting before.' A worried frown creased her wide, smooth brow.

'I'd listen to her story before you tell her off,' he observed casually.

The unspoken overtones almost jumped out and bit her on the nose. 'Why do you say that?' she asked suspiciously. 'Has she said something to you?' The idea of Charlie confiding in someone who was almost a total stranger— Heavens, I'm jealous! she realised. When did I get so sour and disgustingly twisted?

'Sometimes it's easier to talk to someone who's not part of the…'

She could almost see him mentally back-pedalling.

'Part of the problem?' she finished grimly.

'She's very protective of you.'

'You've got to tell me now, Ben.'

Benedict sighed, looked into her lovely face. which was flushed with emotion and tight with tension, and nodded. 'Granted. It seems they had this lesson at school where everyone gave a potted biography of their father. When it was Charlie's turn, she told everyone her father came from a sperm bank.'

'She *what*?'

'I take it this information didn't come from the horse's mouth?'

'What do you think I am?' she gasped.

'It's what Charlie thinks that's the problem.'

'And *you* know what she thinks?' She didn't even bother to hide her antagonism to the idea.

'Don't kill the messenger, Rachel. Shall I make the tea?' he offered, after looking at her pale, drawn features.

'Why not?' She was redundant in every other way—why shouldn't he take over the domestic tasks too? She knew she was being ungrateful and petulant but for the life of her she couldn't stop it.

'This particular boy started making some nasty insinuations about your…er…sexual preferences and, as I said, Charlie's very protective.'

Rachel closed her eyes and groaned; it got worse. 'She's never asked about her father.' If she had what would I have told her? she thought. How would I have explained about Raoul?

'Didn't he want to be involved...?'

'He's dead,' she said in a flat, emotionless tone.

'I see.'

Rachel lifted her elbows from the counter and straightened up, glancing at Benedict as she did so. What did he see? A tragedy that had separated young lovers? Whatever he thought it couldn't come close to the truth.

Had she let that youthful disillusionment sour her attitude to men? Where she'd imagined she was cautious had she actually been distrustful? Had she encumbered her daughter with her own prejudices and insecurities? Had she taken self-reliance too far? The disquieting questions refused to stop.

'My confidence in my parenting skills has just taken a nosedive.'

'Don't knock what you've done, Rachel. Charlie's an exceptional kid. It must have been hard alone...'

'I wasn't alone,' she put in impatiently. 'The money I inherited from my aunt Janet meant I can live here in relative luxury—not up to your standards possibly, but most people wouldn't complain. When Charlie was small Aunt Janet was always there for us. It was she who made me continue with my education; I had it easy compared to a lot of single mums. I had a safety net...'

'And a sense of proportion?'

'What?' She faltered; he looked disconcertingly bored.

'Don't you think you're going a bit overboard with the unfit parent stuff?' he drawled.

'That's rich coming from you,' she gasped incredulously. 'You've only just finished telling me all the things I'm doing wrong!'

'Rachel, what I know about childcare could be fitted on the back of a postage stamp. Of course I'm going to tell you you should be expanding your social horizons; it's in my best interests. We both know I've got an ulterior motive.'

'You have?' Responding at this point might be construed as encouragement but the words that trembled on the tip of her tongue wouldn't be censored.

'I want to be your lover, Rachel.'

'Just like that?' she choked. She'd steeled herself for something much cleverer and more subtle. The simple brutality of the truth was totally devastating. She knew her colour was fluctuating in tune with the violent changes in body temperature she could feel taking place. 'You're very sure of yourself.' It was more a croak than an indignant sneer, but it was the best she could do.

'The only thing I'm sure of, Rachel, is that we'd be good together—*very* good.' Her seared nervous system reacted as violently to his husky tone as if it had been a caress.

'Nigel...'

'Oh, yes, Nigel,' he mused. 'I think you should tell Nigel it's over, don't you?'

Her mouth opened but no sound emerged. His arrogance was literally breathtaking. 'Why should I do that?' It didn't matter a jot that she'd known since the night he proposed that the days of her comfortable relationship with Nigel were numbered. What right did Benedict have to instruct her?

'I'd prefer exclusive rights...'

'To what—my body?' She sucked in air wrathfully. 'I'm no radical feminist but that's the most outrageous thing anyone has *ever*...'

'You might not be political, but you *are* the most stubbornly independent female I've ever met.'

'You mean I don't hang on your every word.'

'Don't get me wrong; I like independent. I'm all for a girl taking the initiative,' he purred suggestively.

This unsubtle reminder of her earlier lapse made her set her chin stubbornly despite her flaming cheeks. 'One kiss and you take a lot for granted. You get exclusive rights to my body and I get what…? Nigel wants to marry me…' She let her words trail off provocatively. That ought to send him running; the prospect didn't make her feel as happy as it should have.

'I'm not proposing.' He didn't appear as intimidated by the suggestion as she'd expected—he didn't seem fazed at all.

'You *do* surprise me,' she snapped sarcastically. 'Tell me, do women usually do exactly what you tell them? They must do; nothing else could account for your incredible arrogance.'

'I gave up comparing you to the other females of my acquaintance within the first thirty seconds of meeting you. Fortunately I like a challenge. I like you.'

'You do?'

'Don't sound so surprised, Rachel. Of course I like you. If you give it half a chance you might find I'm not totally without redeeming features.'

'I don't have time in my life for—complications.' Or heartbreak, she thought, firming her weakening resolve.

'So you admit I'm a complication.'

'We don't want the same things out of life, Ben.'

His mouth thinned and an unexpected spark of anger smouldered to life in his eyes. 'And when did you become such an expert on what I want out of life?'

She stared at him, perplexed by his obvious annoyance. 'I'm not. I couldn't be, could I? You never tell me anything.' As she warmed to her theme his anger seemed all the more perverse. 'You're very clever at worming personal information out of me, but what do I know about you?' Her expansive gesture sent a copper pan suspended decoratively on the wall clattering noisily to the floor. 'A big fat zero. But if office gossip is anything to go by your life follows a fairly predictable pattern.'

'All you had to do was ask. For you I'm an open book. What *do* they say about me on the office grapevine?'

'Depends on who you're talking to—male or female,' she responded sweetly. She wasn't about to bolster his already inflated ego.

'Ouch!' He winced, with a grin.

'I'm taking Charlie her drink,' she announced, turning her back firmly on him and this disturbingly intimate conversation.

CHAPTER FOUR

'AND then Mum kissed him. They thought I was asleep...'

'Charlie!'

'Oh, hiya, Mum. I let Nigel in. You didn't hear the door-bell. I expect you and Ben were—'

'That's enough, Charlie; go to your room!' Rachel said quietly. The tone in her mother's voice made the animated expression fade from her daughter's face.

'But...'

'Now!'

The expression of hurt incomprehension on Nigel's face was making her feel like a bitch—which, looked at from his perspective, she was! He looked like a man whose belief in Santa Claus had been dashed.

She couldn't really lay the blame at Charlie's door, even though she was under no illusions that there had been anything artless about those confidences. She ought to have confessed her true feelings or lack of them sooner. With the ruthlessness of the very young Charlie had seized on the opportunity to get rid of someone she disliked irrespective of the hurt she might be inflicting.

'Do you want me to stay?'

Rachel raised her eyes to Benedict who had entered the room in her wake. 'I don't think so,' she said quietly. That would be rubbing salt in the wound.

'My God!' Nigel got to his feet, an expression of incredulity contorting his regular features. 'He's the thug with the attitude...the barrister you're working for.' His gaze slid from Benedict's impassive features to Rachel's face, which

70

was coloured by a guilty flush. 'Black leather and role-playing...I didn't know sick games like that turned you on, Rachel.'

The contempt in his voice made her feel grubby and if possible even guiltier. 'It was just a coincidence, Nigel.'

His scornful laugh rang out. 'Please; I may not be one of life's intellectual giants, but give me some credit. I don't believe in coincidences.'

What could she say? Neither had she a few days before. Rachel clasped her hands in distress. She hadn't wanted it to end like this. Why, oh, why had she let things drag on? Why, oh, why had she kissed Ben? A thousand 'whys' rushed through her mind.

'I don't suppose you *didn't want to rush things* with him.' He looked at her with fastidious distaste as he caricatured her tone.

'Ben and I—we're not... I mean, we haven't...' She looked to the tall, silent figure at her side for inspiration.

'Yet. We haven't *yet*, sweetheart,' Benedict said, clarifying the point helpfully.

'*Thank you!*' she snapped from between clenched teeth. He was probably enjoying this.

'I'm just glad I found out now, before it was too late, what sort of woman you actually are. I was prepared to make allowances for youthful indiscretion.'

Rachel stiffened at this patronising allusion to her daughter. Benedict's arm moved lightly around her waist and she was grateful for the contact. His splayed fingertips moved over the bony prominence of her hip. The slow, sensuous, soothing movement took the edge off her anxiety. It did a lot of other things too, which, given the circumstances, said a lot about her susceptibility to this man.

'If I'd known your tastes ran to perversions...'

Nigel's thin lips curled as he openly sneered at her and

Rachel's temper flared. Guilt would only compel her to accept so much. Perversions indeed!

'I'm sorry if I've hurt you, Nigel, but that's just plain ridiculous and you know it! I can't marry you, Nigel. I should have told you.'

'Do you think I'd want *you*?' He gaped at her as if she were mad. 'I'm just glad now that we've never slept together...'

That was just in case Ben had missed the previous hints, she decided, repressing a groan.

'You and me both,' Benedict murmured softly in her ear. He tucked a strand of soft brown hair behind her ear and sent a jolt of neat, toe-curling electricity all the way to her feet.

Nigel's eyes were riveted jealously on the apparently intimate gesture. 'I thought you were something special,' he spat. 'I put you on a pedestal. I can see now that Jenny was right about you.'

'Jenny?'

'She's Ted Wilson's cousin. She was very sympathetic on Tuesday.'

'The Tuesday you had a cold.'

'If you must know I felt we needed some time apart for...'

'You to sulk?' she suggested. 'And regale the dinner party with my shortcomings?'

'I didn't know the half of it then.'

It was something about the defensive note in his voice that made her gasp suddenly. 'Is it possible that you've been seeing this sympathetic person? What was her name?'

She'd always accepted work commitments as the reason for him pulling out of a number of arrangements at the last minute. Now it looked suspiciously as if he had been keeping his options open all along!

'Jenny,' he responded, tight-lipped, looking annoyed that she'd introduced the subject. 'It's all perfectly innocent.'

'Is that what you told her about us?' The unattractive shade of crimson that washed over his fair complexion was more revealing than any words.

'I asked you to marry me,' he responded in a disgruntled tone.

'Flip the coin again.' She felt a whole lot less wretched knowing that Nigel wasn't the saint she'd thought him.

'Promiscuous women like you are ten-a-penny, and then these days there's the question of contamination simply on medical grounds.'

'That's it.' Benedict's voice was suddenly decisive. 'A bit of bile is acceptable when you've just been kicked where it hurts, but I think Rachel has grovelled guiltily for long enough. Cut your losses, mate, and clear out.' His tone was unfailingly polite but the hard light of warning in his dark eyes told another story. 'Don't be tempted to indulge in any more colourful insults or I might just be tempted to—'

This intervention was too much! Rachel pulled clear of his arms. 'I'm quite capable of sorting out my own problems.'

He shrugged and held up his hands in mock submission. 'I never thought otherwise.' His smile held a caressing warmth that robbed her anger of its impetus.

She cleared her throat. 'Good.' She grabbed her scattered wits by the scruff of the neck. 'Nigel...'

'Don't worry, I'm going. I can see how things are.' He looked from Rachel to the tall man at her side. 'I'm not blind. Don't bother—I know my way out,' he said bitterly. The slamming of the front door reverberated through the flat.

'Poor Nigel.'

'Don't become too attached to that hair shirt, Rachel; it doesn't suit you. *Poor* Nigel has a filthy mind and a substitute in the wings—crafty old Nigel..'

'He's not like that, really; he was hurt and humiliated.'

Benedict found her defence of her former lover irritating,

though it seemed the 'lover' part hadn't been strictly accurate.

'Why didn't you sleep with him?'

'Is it obligatory?' She could hardly tell him she was a cautious individual with a low sex drive after the way she'd behaved with him!

'When you're going to marry someone it usually is,' he confirmed drily.

'I didn't say yes.'

'He mentioned that.'

'I mean I didn't say I'd marry him.'

'Didn't he think it was a bit odd?' Benedict continued with what she considered insensitive persistence.

'He was sensitive and understanding.'

'Dead from the neck down, more like!'

'You can be very coarse and vulgar,' she observed frigidly.

'I can,' he promised warmly.

The warmth as much as the promise made her step backwards. The impetuous movement brought her into direct collision with a coffee table over which she fell in a tangle of arms and legs.

'Don't touch me!' she commanded urgently as he bent forward. 'I can't think when you touch me.'

'That's the nicest thing you've ever said to me,' he told her as she got to her feet, straightened the coffee table and wished she'd been wearing trousers. She smoothed her skirt with slightly unsteady fingers.

'Well, cherish it because that's as good as it's going to get,' she said nastily.

'I cherish every kind word you say to me, Rachel, and a few of the insulting ones too.'

An unwilling laugh was torn from her throat; he was impossible! Shaking her head slowly from side to side as she looked reprovingly at him dislodged the last remaining hairpin and her gently waving, glossy hair cascaded slowly around her face.

'Blast!' she cried impatiently as the heavy weight came to rest at shoulder-blade level.

'Is it as soft as it looks?'

The tone of his voice as much as the taut, hungry expression on his face warned her of the imminent danger of this situation. She turned a deaf ear to the reckless voice that told her to walk straight into the path of that danger. Nothing in her life had prepared her for the physical pain of denial.

'I think you should go too, Ben. I'm very grateful for your help today.' Both the wanted and the unwanted, she thought, but now wasn't the time to quibble. 'I'm tired; I want to go to bed.' The sudden wicked gleam in his eyes made her rush on swiftly. 'And I need to talk to Charlie,' she said with as much dignity as she could muster.

Dignity wasn't usually something she had to work at—she had buckets full of the stuff. Calm, unruffled composure was her trademark; she knew it, and liked it. It kept unwanted attention at bay. What had happened to her? She wasn't the sort of girl who needed a shoulder, strong or otherwise, to lean on. She wasn't the sort of girl who kissed unsuitable men who looked on women as a way to pass a few hours pleasurably.

'About her father?'

'I don't know,' she said honestly. 'I imagine we'll touch on artificial insemination,' she said drily. It was time for the 'warm loving relationship' speech and she wasn't looking forward to it. It that area she hadn't been the best role model in the world.

'And us?'

'I'll see you in the office tomorrow,' she replied, deliberately misunderstanding him.

'With your hair neatly secured...I know,' he said, his tone

laden with an irony that brought a self-conscious flush to her cheeks. At the door he turned abruptly. 'Wear your hair loose for me tomorrow, Rachel,' he said impetuously.

She was still digesting this ludicrous request when he left, his departure a good deal quieter than Nigel's. Wear my hair loose indeed, she snorted. What exactly would he make of it if she did? He'd see it as some sort of silent admission—a surrender.

Surrender... A sudden shudder racked her slim body and she was conscious of her aching breasts and the way they chafed against the white shirt she wore. She'd be mad to pander to his private fantasies; it was all about control and domination and she wasn't about to buy into that sort of thing—not for a minute!

Her confrontation with Charlie was delayed until the morning. When she entered her daughter's room she was sprawled face down across the bed. Rachel removed her shoes and pulled the quilt over her before telephoning the neighbour who looked after Charlie for the couple of hours after school before she finished work. Fortunately she was happy to have her the next day. She'd have loved to stay at home the next day, but being a working mother, she'd already discovered, required a lot of compromise.

Benedict's eyes went immediately to his secretary's desk as he walked into the outer office. The morning sun fell directly onto the corner from where the efficient hum of the word processor issued.

'Good morning.' Rachel cradled a phone against her cheek. 'Your father rang; he's on his way down.'

Not even the royal visitation could cloud this morning. Benedict nodded. 'Thank you, Rachel.'

Rachel would have known his appreciation wasn't directed at her ability to convey a message even if his eyes hadn't been fixed on the cloud of hair which rippled over her shoulders.

She'd almost been late this morning. First she'd gone all the way back to the flat to pin up her hair, then there had been the last-minute visit to the ladies' room to demolish her previous efforts.

Why shouldn't a girl change her hairstyle if she wanted? If Benedict wanted to read anything into it that was his problem. She could rationalise as much as she liked, but she'd still been waiting with baited breath for his arrival. He'd been pleased, if the savage satisfaction that had flared in his dark eyes could be interpreted as pleasure.

'How's Charlie this morning?'

'She sends her love.' This was the literal and worrying truth.

'Is anything the matter?'

His perception was as acute as ever. I don't want my daughter to get too fond of you, would have sounded churlish, but it was true. From their conversation earlier this morning she'd noticed that Charlie was exhibiting a dangerous tendency to attach the label 'father figure' around Benedict's neck.

She'd tried tactfully to discourage this development, but she was gloomily aware that her words hadn't fallen on fertile ground. Her own heart would have to take care of itself but she didn't want to take similar risks with her daughter's. She had no right to throw caution to the winds.

Her fingers suddenly itched to twist her hair into a neat knot. What am I doing? she thought angrily. I might as well pin a sign around my neck saying 'Just whistle'! Talk about a pushover!

Stuart Arden didn't make a habit of knocking and Rachel was taken completely unawares, and, if the expression on his face was anything to go by, so was Benedict.

The sudden sight of the very slim, very tall, very *young* blonde throwing her arms around Benedict's neck was a traumatic shock to her system. If she'd had a pair of scissors handy she might just have hacked off her hair at that moment and left him to make what he would of that symbolism.

Sir Stuart Arden, looking every inch the powerful pillar of the community, stood back with an expression of approval on his face.

'I thought I'd surprise you with Sabrina,' he said as his son emerged from the thorough embrace.

'Gift-wrapped, I see.' Benedict's expression didn't give away anything, but Rachel was pretty sure he didn't object to this form of greeting—what man would?

'Do you like it, darling?'

Rachel observed the crimson fingertips and the lime-green and lilac striped sheath dress with distaste. She was the sort of girl who called everyone 'darling' indiscriminately. Only in Benedict's case she probably meant it. Her proprietorial air with him spoke of a close relationship. The thought of how close made Rachel feel nauseous.

'I hope they charged you by the yard,' he observed, eyeing the length of leg revealed.

'Try and think metric, darling. I was telling your father, I've hardly seen you since you got back from that horrid farm.' She pouted attractively up at him.

Rachel, who had seen exactly where his masculine gaze was resting, would have bet money that that hateful laugh had been practised for hours to get that perfect sexy intonation.

'Considering the amount of time you've spent behind a desk, Benedict, I was quite surprised.'

Rachel was immediately conscious, despite the casual tone, of the tension in the air between father and son. Aware that his absence yesterday had been on her account, she hoped this wasn't responsible for the friction.

'Have you, or any clients, got any complaints about my work?' Benedict already knew the answer. His father was no sentimentalist.

He had never made any secret of the fact that he wanted one of his sons to carry on the family tradition of heading the prestigious law firm which had been founded by their great-grandfather, but it had been shrewd judgement rather than nepotism that explained Benedict's presence.

He was here because he was the best of his year's crop of law graduates and this firm always wanted the best. He'd refused offers from rival law chambers and his father knew it, although he never referred to the fact.

'You'd know if I had,' Stuart Arden confirmed. 'I was talking to your father last night, Sabrina; he was telling me you've graduated with flying colours from your cordon bleu course.'

'I was going to practise my skills on Benedict.' She glanced upwards through her heavily mascaraed lashes at him.

I just bet you were, Rachel thought with a fresh spurt of self-disgust. What am I doing? I don't want any part in this tacky scenario. I'm not going to compete for a man's attentions like this; it's so demeaning.

'Only he stood me up,' Sabrina continued with a sigh. She tapped his hand playfully. 'I was devastated. Did Daddy tell you he's going to set me up in my own little catering firm?'

'Well, if we can put any work your way...'

That was how it worked, Rachel thought, when you knew the right people—so simple. This was Benedict's world, not hers; the gap between them had never been more apparent. Her hands were clammy as she struck the keyboard and tried to pretend she wasn't listening to every word. To the Sir

Stuarts and Sabrinas of this world secretaries were just part of the furniture. They probably hadn't even noticed she was there. However, the next words blew a big hole in this theory.

'You're not Maggie.'

'Pardon?' She didn't immediately realise that this remark was addressed to her. 'No, I'm not.' The great man stood waiting expectantly and she knew she was looking more and more foolish with each passing second, but her vocal cords had seized up.

'I thought you arranged the temporary transfer, Father.' Benedict came unexpectedly to her rescue.

'Did I? I do a lot of things around this place.'

'And with your failing faculties you can't be expected to recall them all,' Benedict observed in an understanding manner.

'You're such a tease,' Sabrina remonstrated. 'I wish half the so-called *young* men I know had half Sir Stuart's energy and dynamism.'

Rachel had never understood why intelligent men who had given up reading fairy tales years ago fell for such blatant flattery. It works every time, she thought, watching the distinguished-looking peer try to hide his pleasure. He puffed out his not insubstantial chest.

'I only popped in to invite you out to lunch. You will come, won't you, darling Ben?'

That endearment had the same effect on Rachel's nerve-endings as a dentist's drill. She clenched her teeth and bent blindly over her desk, giving a passable imitation of intense concentration.

'Sorry, but I'll have to take a rain-check, Sabrina. I've got something else on.'

'Anyone I know?' she enquired archly, and the Cupid's-bow mouth tightened noticeably.

'Let me walk you out.'

'I'll wait for you in the office, Benedict. Perhaps Mrs French could get me some coffee?'

'Miss French.' She wondered with a spurt of militancy what he'd say if she pointed out that coffee-making wasn't included in her job description.

'*Miss* French.' He inclined his leonine head slightly as he moved past her. 'I stand corrected.' And that didn't happen too often, she surmised, repressing an inappropriate urge to laugh—obviously nerves. 'Are you enjoying working for my son? Is he a considerate boss?' he enquired casually.

'It's nice to have an opportunity to use my linguistic skills.' Rachel had the distinct impression that nothing this man said was unplanned.

'Very diplomatic. I've heard you're a *clever* young woman.' Rachel frowned. The way he'd said 'clever' sounded almost like an insult. 'I have a friend who works in Brussels who's always on the look-out for people with your sort of expertise in languages. You'd be in great demand over there.'

Suddenly he knew a lot about her, she thought as she smiled noncommittally back.

'Have you ever thought about moving?'

'I have a child, Sir Stuart.'

'Boarding-school's the answer; it makes them independent. Our lot thrived on it. I take my coffee black,' he added abruptly as he stalked into Benedict's office.

This sudden concern for her future rang alarms bells in Rachel's head. What was behind this interest? She suddenly didn't feel at all comfortable.

'This is for my father, I take it?'

Rachel wondered whether he ever dropped the formal 'father'. She nodded.

'I'll take it in.' Benedict took the cup from her hand. 'An urgent call in...' he glanced at his watch '...shall we say

seven minutes? Don't look so shocked, Rachel; where do you
think I learnt my tactics?'

Rachel stared as he closed the interconnecting door. Being
orphaned too early to recall her parents hadn't made her the
world's leading expert on family dynamics, but what
Benedict had with his father didn't seem like your typical
father-son relationship.

Stuart Arden had seated himself behind his son's desk. The
gesture was inspired more by habit than a belief that it would
help him intimidate his son; he knew his offspring too well
for that. Benedict's independence had been an infuriating
characteristic even when he was a baby. He often thought
he'd got all his elder brother's share. The only time Tom had
ever shown any backbone was when he'd refused to take his
bar exams and follow in his father's footsteps.

'What can I do for you, Father?' Benedict placed the cup
down on the desk and strolled towards the window. He didn't
notice the small red light that indicated his father had
switched on the intercom.

'There's been talk. Talk about you and that French
woman.'

'You must have been listening hard to hear any *talk*,'
Benedict observed sceptically.

'Something's been wrong with you since you got back and
you left the office with her yesterday and cancelled all your
afternoon appointments. It doesn't take much imagination...'

'Not much, just a particular type.' Benedict spoke without
any discernible inflection. Head slightly inclined to one side,
eyes narrowed, he moved across the room and looked at his
father thoughtfully. 'So you pulled her file and scurried down
here to check her out. Her name is Rachel.' Benedict was
too familiar with his parent's *modus operandi* to sound surprised by this discovery.

'There's a company policy about that sort of thing.'

'That's a new one on me,' Benedict observed with interest.

'Are you sleeping with her?'

'Is this exchange of intimacies meant to bring us closer? I hate to disappoint you but I've already got a best friend to share my secrets with.'

'Huh! Share, *you*? That I don't believe; you've never voluntarily given away any information in your life. You always were the most evasive child...'

'I was only being polite,' Benedict admitted. 'You know me so well. ''Mind your own business'' sounded so...bald and lacking in respect.'

Stuart Arden gritted his teeth. Benedict was the one who was meant to be on the defensive. He tapped his fingers impatiently on the desk. That infuriatingly languid tone of Benedict's always irritated him—he did it deliberately, of course...

'She works for you, she has a child... You're going to raise...false expectations; of course she's eager. I'm not saying she's set out deliberately to snare you.'

'That's very generous of you.'

'You can sneer, Benedict, but you have to look at the facts. In her position who could blame her for...? You're a *catch*, so they tell me. You'll make her a figure of fun when you've finished with her.'

'What an exemplary employer you are,' Benedict breathed admiringly. 'So considerate towards your employees. I'm curious about your sources. Is this fatherly instinct or surveillance talking now?' The resigned humour had been replaced by a definite thread of hard anger, but his father continued, oblivious to the change.

'Why go looking for trouble when there are any number of suitable young things like Serena...?'

'Sabrina,' Benedict corrected him drily.

'Whatever.' His father brushed aside the interruption im-

patiently. 'The right sort of wife is very important for someone in our position. If you'd been married you wouldn't have
been so eager to spend six months sorting out a manager for
that damned property. I'm sure she only left you the place
to spite me!' he added in a disgruntled tone.

'Knowing Gran, you're probably right,' Benedict conceded
with a sudden grin. 'I'm surprised you married Mum, considering her shaky pedigree. The word hypocrite springs to
mind for some reason.'

'That's entirely different.'

'It would be, of course. But have I got this right? The
consensus is I should marry...sooner rather than later. How
do you know I'm not considering it...?' Even though his
only intention when he'd opened his mouth had been to taunt
his father, by the time he closed it a number of things had
fallen into place in his mind.

'*You*, lumbered with another man's cast-off?'

'Are we talking child or mother here?' Benedict let this
slur pass unpunished. His heart wasn't wholly committed to
the verbal combat any longer; he was still reeling from an
unexpected discovery.

'Both! It would be social suicide. Have you any idea how
many skeletons a woman like her is bound to have? A High
Court judge needs to have a blemishless background...'

An unwilling laugh was torn from Benedict's throat. 'High
Court judge! So that's what I want to be when I grow up, is
it, *Daddy*?'

'You've got a brilliant future ahead of you; everyone says
so,' his father said defensively, aware that he'd gone further
than he intended in the heat of the moment.

'Thank you, Father.' A smile that worried his parent no
end curved the stern outline of Benedict's lips.

Feeling old, the elder man levered himself slowly from the
leather swivel chair. 'Thank me for what?' he said suspi-

ciously. Emily had warned him to leave well alone. You'd think he'd have learnt by now—his wife usually knew what she was talking about, he reflected grimly.

'For reminding me it's *my* life.'

'My life? What sort of talk is that? You're an Arden, boy; you're my heir.'

'So long as I toe the line?' Benedict suggested lightly. 'You've got other children.'

'Your brother is happy being a country solicitor.' He shook his head, unable to comprehend how his first-born was happy with such an existence.

'Nat...'

'Natalie is a girl.'

'Open your eyes. Nat is a girl with enough drive and ambition to light up the national grid; is a girl who is as well endowed in the brains department as me.'

'Did she gain entrance to Oxford when she was—?'

'Oh, I know she hasn't gone through school three years ahead of her peers, but that's only because you didn't think it worthwhile to constantly urge her onwards and upwards—she being a mere girl.'

'You didn't complain!'

'Maybe you don't know what things are really important until it's too late,' Benedict observed thoughtfully. He wasn't assigning blame. So certain aspects of his childhood might have been better—the same could be said for a large proportion of the population. He was much more interested in the present.

'I tell you something, Father, you really should take a good look at Nat one of these days—you might be pleasantly surprised. She's certainly hungry to prove herself to you.'

'Unlike you.' He sounded disgruntled but Benedict could see his father was looking thoughtful. 'About that woman...'

'Rachel,' Benedict said firmly.

'I'm only thinking of your best interests.'

'A twelve-bore might be less destructive than your concern,' Benedict told him frankly but without heat. 'If it makes you feel any better she isn't interested in me...'

His father laughed ruefully. 'Perhaps she's got something about her after all.'

'Parental approval—I feel *so* much better.'

'I'll thank you to keep a civil tongue in your head, young man, and I'm not approving of anything.'

'Were you rude to her?'

'As a matter of fact I was extremely civil.'

'Oh?'

The narrow-eyed suspicion from his offspring provoked an exasperated sigh. 'It's possible I might have accidentally flicked on the intercom whilst we were...'

'Whilst *you* were calling her a gold-digging opportunist. I suppose you made sure she received a strictly expurgated version.'

'Naturally when I happened to see the red light I switched it off.'

Giving his father a hawkish look that shook the older man deeply, Benedict turned his back and strode purposefully out of the room.

Surprise, surprise, the outer office was empty. He couldn't go back into his office; he didn't trust himself to look at his father, let alone speak to him. He'd been entirely too tolerant of the manipulative old man over the years.

Where would she go? he wondered. Her half-opened bag lay beside the desk. Of course—the answer was obvious. Where did women always go when they wanted to shed a tear in private?

'Good morning, Ben.' The latest female pupil to be recruited to the chambers stared at him, startled, as he walked confidently past her into the ladies' room.

'Morning, Sarah.'

A quick survey revealed there was nobody standing beside the mirrors that ran the length of the plushly carpeted room. One cubicle door was closed.

'I know you're in there, Rachel, so you might as well come out. You only heard what my father wanted you to.' His voice echoed in the high-ceilinged room. 'I know you can hear me, Rachel. I need to talk to you. Come on out. Damn it, woman, if you don't come out I'll knock the door down!' he warned.

His head fell back as relief flooded through his body at the sound of the bolt sliding back. 'Rach—' The eager smile faded dramatically from his face as the occupant fully emerged.

'Sorry to disappoint you, Ben, but it's only me.' A solicitor with whom he'd worked on several occasions stepped forward, trying without much success to hide her broad grin.

'Carol. Hello. I thought you were someone else.'

'So I gathered,' she observed, with a limpid look. 'I had no idea you were so romantic...or forceful...' A twinge of envy mingled with her amusement as she finally succumbed to mirth, but she was talking to empty space.

CHAPTER FIVE

'SORRY I'm late.'

Kurt Hassler got to his feet, his hand extended. 'Don't worry, Ben; Rachel explained about your emergency. We've been well looked after.'

'I'm sure you have.'

Rachel's eyes slid self-consciously away from the dark, ironic gaze. 'I'll see you all after lunch, gentlemen,' she said with a smile as she got to her feet.

'It's a working lunch; I think it would be beneficial to have you with us, Rachel. Besides, it's going to be a long session this afternoon; we don't want you fading on us before we're through.' He turned to the other men. 'These young women and their apples and yogurt. Always dieting.' There was a general male wave of agreement and a flurry of compliments on the perfection of her figure.

Rachel's smile became strained as she thought vicious thoughts about where she'd put her apple had she had one to hand. She was sure that Ben knew exactly how much she hated this patronising, pat-her-on-the-head sort of situation.

'I don't diet and I've never had any complaints about my staying power.' She positioned herself between the solid bulk of Kurt Hassler and Benedict. 'However, there's no way I'm going to turn down a free lunch.'

There was also no way she was going to let Benedict know she'd heard the start of the humiliating conversation with his father. At least she could stop worrying about the possibility that she was going to cave in to temptation. After the things Sir Stuart had said she had no doubt Ben would steer clear of her. A dalliance with a mere secretary—especially one, horror of horrors, with a child!—wasn't worth risking his brilliant prospects for.

And after that afternoon she had no doubt he had a brilliant future. He had cut a path through the legal maze which had made Albert despair. The clients went away happy, knowing they'd been saved a very costly court battle, and she could go home knowing her stint as Benedict Arden's PA was going to be much shorter than she'd anticipated.

'So you're still here?'

'Ask the same question in ten seconds and you'll be talking to fresh air,' she promised, heaving her bag onto her shoulder. 'You must be pleased with how things went today.'

'What happened to my seven-minute phone call?' Benedict growled unexpectedly. He sat down on the deep window seat and she thought he looked to be in a foul humour for someone who'd just achieved miracles.

Calmly she buttoned her dark tailored jacket to the neck. The very precise way she did so seemed to irritate him—his irritation was hard to miss. Some perverse imp made her go back and flick off an invisible speck then smooth a sleeve once more.

'Albert's temp was having a problem this morning locating a brief,' she explained, with a final glance around her clean desk. 'You don't mind that I slipped down to help, do you?'

'Why should I mind?'

'You look a bit…on edge,' she observed innocently. She met his hard scrutiny with a bland indifference that gave no hint of the churning misery in her stomach. Was he seeing the same scheming bitch his father evidently did when he looked at her now? Was he wishing he'd never shown any interest?

'On edge,' he mused. 'That's as good a description as

any.' For some reason the thought seemed to amuse him. 'Are you surprised? You've met my father...'

'On several occasions,' she admitted, compressing her lips. 'I didn't know I'd made a deep impression, but today he seemed to know an awful lot about me.'

'You did hear, didn't you? Look at me, Rachel,' Benedict said, and she could hear the urgency in his voice.

'Hear what?' she said in a bewildered tone.

'You heard what my father said—heard what he *intended* you to hear. Didn't you?'

'It's no big deal,' she said, making a big show of looking at her watch. 'What I did hear made very good sense.'

What a fool she'd been to imagine she'd ever been anything but a passing fancy. Men like Ben Arden didn't take women like her seriously—she was a novelty to a jaded palate, that was all. She ought to be thanking Stuart Arden for making her wake up.

Walking through the corridors of the old, luxuriously furnished building today, she'd been hard-pressed not to assume that every quiet conversation she came upon was about her. Rationality didn't come into it; the seeds of doubt had been planted and she felt conspicuous, as though everyone knew about her lustful fantasies. Fantasies that had almost become reality.

When he spoke Benedict's deep voice vibrated with anger and frustration. 'You and my father are on the same wavelength, it would seem.' His nostrils flared and the sensual curve of his lips was outlined by a thin white rim of anger. He came around and placed his hands palm down on her desk. The sturdy oak trembled slightly under the pressure, but not nearly as much as her knees trembled.

'Do you mind?' she asked coldly, catching hold of the creased corner of a document under his hand.

As he leaned forward the warm male smell of his body

assaulted her nostrils. She could see the faint dark blur of body hair through the fine white cotton of his shirt. Despite the air-conditioned coolness of the room sweat trickled down the valley between her breasts. Her hostility was almost submerged by the scorching thrill of arousal that swept through her.

With a sweeping movement he knocked the whole pile she was attempting to straighten onto the floor. 'Will you stop that?'

For a moment she'd thought he had been privy to her prohibited thoughts. The flush of mortification faded when she recognised his meaning.

'It's what I'm paid to do!' She hadn't even realised she'd been sharpening a pile of pencils that lay neatly on her desk. 'You won't get anywhere with me by acting like a thwarted child!'

The veneer of indifference was abruptly torn away and suddenly she was trembling with suppressed emotion—with humiliation. What did he think it felt like to hear herself discussed like a...an object? He might not like being reminded that at the end of the day it was daddy who called the shots, but at least he hadn't heard himself spoken of like some sort of grasping tart!

'How will I get somewhere with you?' The husky query made her quiver.

This was a question she decided it was politic to avoid. 'Why didn't he just sack me?' she wondered out loud. She bit down firmly on her trembling lower lip.

'Because that would leave him open to an accusation of unfair dismissal,' Benedict said gently. He didn't doubt his father would have used this method had it been an option.

'I hope you told him he had nothing to worry about. A kiss, a bit of mild flirtation...I'm sure you're much more pragmatic than he thinks. It would certainly take more than me to distract you from your great future.'

'I'm much more selfish than either of you think.'

She didn't quite know what to make of this cryptic utterance, and mysteriously Benedict's expression wasn't showing much of the relief she'd expected after she'd so generously let him off the hook. She didn't think for a minute he'd consider the effort of continuing to pursue her would be worth the aggravation.

Her slender shoulders lifted fractionally and she gave a brittle laugh. 'I'd hate to be the cause of dissent.'

'Dissent is the natural state between my father and me.'

'Fine, if that suits you, but I don't feel happy being in the middle of your private battleground.' Her eyes filled slowly with tears and angrily she blinked back the stinging heat. 'Hearing you discuss me…it made me feel soiled and…' She shook her head as she swallowed the constriction in her throat.

'Hurt,' Benedict supplied gently.

'No matter,' she said with a sniff. Hurt implied she cared to begin with. 'I know some people think just being a single parent automatically means that you're on the look-out to rectify the situation.' She swallowed and cleared her throat. Losing her cool now wasn't going to help. 'About lunch; shall I book you a table for two for tomorrow?' She could be the perfect secretary for a few more days, maybe less— how hard could it be?

'What makes you think I'll need a table for two?'

'I thought you might want to lunch with Sabrina; she did leave a message to that effect. Didn't you get it?'

'I did.'

'She looks a very persuasive sort of girl.' Perhaps I can take night classes in eyelash-fluttering, she thought viciously as she smiled generously.

'She's also a great cook,' he agreed readily. 'It makes you wonder why I settled for an indifferent cheese sandwich instead of the full works, doesn't it? Yes,' he agreed, folding his arms across his chest as she looked up with a startled expression. 'I was on my way there when Charlie kidnapped me. Can you take a letter?'

'Of course,' she replied, her professional dignity stung as she knocked all the neatly sharpened pencils onto the floor.

'It's a letter of resignation,' he continued calmly as she scrabbled about on her knees, retrieving the scattered pencils.

'A what?' she yelped, straightening up and hitting her head on the desk. 'Ouch! You want me to resign?'

'*My* letter of resignation.'

'You can't resign because of me!' she said in a horror-struck tone. She sat back on her heels, wondering how she'd managed to get caught up in the middle of this chaos.

'I'm not resigning because of you.'

'Oh! Of course not.' That's what happens when you get ideas above your station, my girl, she told herself. If the father could humiliate her, why not the son?

'Although I can see that would be quite a gesture.' His frivolous tone made her frown.

'I think you should think very seriously about this, Ben.'

'I know you believe I'm a capricious party animal, incapable of sober reflection.' The ironic flick of his eyes made her flush guiltily. 'But I have actually thought this out. It's something I've been thinking about ever since I came back from Australia. I'm going back...'

And there was me thinking I had something to do with his decision. The dark irony was like a dagger-thrust.

'I see.' It's about time you opened your eyes and did just that, girl, she told herself sternly. 'And how you spend your leisure time is nothing to do with me. You're single, eligible, and it's very natural that you like to let your hair down.'

These pragmatic words succeeded in focusing his eyes on her own hair, which fell softly around her shoulders. 'The London social scene will probably grind to a halt without you,' she added quickly.

'That sounds a bit impersonal; I'd prefer to picture pillows wet with tears.'

I just bet you would, she thought, inhaling deeply to steady herself. 'The world is full of impressionable females.' Her tone made it quite clear she didn't categorise herself as one of these.

She was getting her message across loud and clear. 'Your world might be full of them, but I meet precious few.' Benedict responded drily.

'Perhaps you'll have more luck in the outback?' He was actually serious; it finally filtered into her consciousness. He was going. Would he *really* give up a lifestyle most people would envy?

'Australian women are certainly refreshingly open.'

'Are they the main reason you're going there?'

'Careful, Rachel, you're sounding jealous,' he pointed out smoothly. He ignored her strangled squeak of denial and continued smoothly. 'My grandmother left me a cattle station in Queensland when she died four years ago. I put in a manager and left it to take care of itself until last year when he walked out and it became painfully clear he'd been siphoning off profits.'

'Oh!'

'Oh, indeed, especially as Nina left me land but very little capital. Remember we're talking a different scale; put the station in Britain and think a small village. A lot of people's livelihood depends on its continued prosperity. Overstocking plus drought had left the place in a pretty bad way. I went out to sort out the legal wrangles and put another manager— one I could trust—in his place. If it wasn't for my mother's sentimental attachment to the place—she was brought up on the Creek—I might well have put it on the market. It was just one big hassle.'

'Was?'

Benedict grinned and she realised she'd never seen his eyes burn with quite that sort of enthusiasm before.

'It still is, but the place has a way of getting under your skin. My life has always been so predictable: pass exams before and with higher marks than the next guy; be the first, the best... It stopped being a challenge years ago. Connor's Creek is different; the land is...' He gave an almost self-conscious shrug. 'To cut a long story short I kept putting off finding a manager and in the end I didn't bother.'

'You never intended staying here?' Did I come under the heading of time-filler—a handy stopgap? she wondered bitterly.

'I left my options open.' Deep down he knew that wasn't really true; he'd always known he was going back.

'I can't see you...'

'The suit does come off...remember? I had a hard time convincing the people there I was serious too. Some people go too much on appearances.'

She *did* remember what he looked like without the suit and suddenly it wasn't so hard to think of him getting his hands dirty working under some vast, alien blue sky. She could imagine him relishing shrugging off the constraints of civilisation and undertaking a task that required not just his mental tenacity but also his physical endurance.

'Your family won't be happy.' Why did she feel like this—so *empty*? She was physically attracted to him, nothing else. His leaving was a perfect solution in many ways to her own problem. No Benedict—no problem.

'Dad's got an heir apparent; he just doesn't realise it yet.'

'What about law—your career?'

'It'll survive without me. To be honest this has always bored me.' His shrug took in their surroundings.

'Perhaps that's why you throw yourself so wholeheartedly into the social whirl—you're compensating for your stifling professional life? Pardon me for saying so, but that all sounds a bit glib. Who's to say you won't get bored with playing cowboy in few years' time?'

'Leave the bitter irony to me, Rachel; it doesn't suit you.' His quiet tone made her feel uncharitable and plain mean. 'Not many people find a place they know they're truly meant to be. When I make up my mind what I want I'm not easily deflected.'

The warning in his words made her shiver. If she didn't tear her eyes away from his, critical meltdown was imminent!

If anyone had told him a year ago that a man could become emotionally attached to a place, a piece of land, he'd have laughed. Now he knew differently. As he'd explored the vast expanse of land they called the Creek he'd found himself envying the men who had settled this area, who'd been the first. This rapport with the land wasn't something he could put into words—wasn't something he could explain to anyone.

'It's a big step to take,' she said huskily.

'They're the only ones worth taking, Rachel.' He extended his hand and she realised she was still sitting on the floor, her fingers clutching a pile of papers. Her hand slid inside his and he pulled her to her feet. With a tiny jerk of his arm he drew her closer and she automatically raised her eyes to his.

It was a mistake. He was going to the other side of the world; it wasn't something she was likely to forget but she thought this was an opportune moment to remind herself of the fact while her nervous system was plugged into its own personal high-voltage system.

NO POSTAGE
NECESSARY
IF MAILED
IN THE
UNITED STATES

BUSINESS REPLY MAIL
FIRST-CLASS MAIL   PERMIT NO. 717   BUFFALO, NY

POSTAGE WILL BE PAID BY ADDRESSEE

**HARLEQUIN READER SERVICE
3010 WALDEN AVE
PO BOX 1867
BUFFALO NY 14240-9952**

GET FREE BOOKS
and a
FREE GIFT WHEN YOU PLAY THE...

LAS VEGAS GAME

Just scratch off the gold box with a coin. Then check below to see the gifts you get!

YES!

I have scratched off the gold Box. Please send me my **2 FREE BOOKS** and **gift for which I qualify.** I understand that I am under no obligation to purchase any books as explained on the back of this card.

▲ DETACH AND MAIL CARD TODAY! ▲

306 HDL DCM7

106 HDL DCMW
(H-P-OS-02/01)

NAME   (PLEASE PRINT CLEARLY)

ADDRESS

APT.#   CITY

STATE/PROV.   ZIP/POSTAL CODE

7	7	7	Worth TWO FREE BOOKS plus a BONUS Mystery Gift!
🍒	🍒	🍒	Worth TWO FREE BOOKS!
🔔	🔔	♣	TRY AGAIN!

He knew how he made her feel—he knew *exactly* how he made her feel; he was too experienced to miss the obvious signs she was transmitting. Walking away from Benedict Arden with her pride intact might be a small step when compared to what he was doing, but it was going to be one of the hardest things she'd ever done.

'Is what you've told me public knowledge, or do you want me to be discreet?'

When she'd tried to step back he'd slid his fingers down to the curve of her elbow. It was stand still and take the agony that being this close to him was giving her or dislocate her shoulder. On reflection maybe dislocations weren't that bad!

'You're the only person I've told.' She could feel the web of intimacy his soft words were weaving around her. Illusion, she told herself—wishful thinking. 'Will you be sorry to see me go, Rachel?'

'I'm only your temporary secretary,' she reminded him lightly. 'It doesn't really affect me.' I'm a temporary everything, she thought with a surge of self-pity.

'I was forgetting,' he said smoothly. His eyes were on the small creamy V of skin where her shirt was modestly unbuttoned at the neck. She half expected the delicate gold chain she wore to melt under the hot, smoky scrutiny. 'And I suppose on a more personal note it might even help my cause.'

'How exactly?' she asked uncertainly. It occurred to her that if anyone walked in right now the gossips would have something more substantial than hearsay to sink their fangs into.

'You don't like the fact that Charlie likes me. You're afraid of her getting attached to me. This way there's no chance of that happening now, is there? I'm just passing through.'

'You always were,' she snapped bitterly. 'And anyway it's not true!' The quirk of one eloquent dark brow made her subside into slightly resentful silence. A mother's job was to protect her child; she refused to feel apologetic.

'It's a natural enough response. You like to keep men on the outside—strictly no admittance to the enchanted circle. That's probably why you took such a shine to good old Nigel—you knew there was no possibility of him cracking the code. I don't think your home has stayed a male-free zone by accident.'

'What a load of rubbish!' she shouted. What was wrong with being emotionally independent? He made it sound like a disease. 'I'm old enough to realise that some relationships are transitory—shallow; Charlie isn't. I don't want her to be hurt. You're nice to her and she's reading all sorts of things into it. She's used to men who run a mile when they know you have a child; she can cope with them.'

'Be serious, Rachel. Look in the mirror.' He took her chin in his hand and examined her profile greedily. 'Most men would put up with a tribe of juvenile delinquents if you were part of the bargain.'

'Most men want a shallow, superficial relationship.' Her defiance was weakening. If he'd chosen that moment to kiss away her objections she'd have been a goner.

'And isn't that exactly what you wanted with *Steve*...me? Didn't you fantasise just a little bit about making love to a total stranger—no questions, no complications? You were attracted to him—me. I've never seen a more obvious case of lust at first sight. Anonymous sex—didn't you think about it? You could safely surrender to male dominance; I'm sure that was tempting. You'd be completely free with a stranger to express your needs in any way you chose.'

The emotions his throaty, insidious words stirred up made

her head spin—with anger, she told herself. 'Sex with a
stranger is not my idea of safety,' she said unsteadily.

'Perhaps a safety valve would be a more appropriate description,' he conceded calmly. 'A release for all your re-
pressed sexual feelings. It wouldn't surprise me if the last
person you slept with was Charlie's father,' he jeered provocatively.

Seeing the expression on her face, he froze. 'Good God!'
he breathed hoarsely. 'It's true, isn't it?' Under the healthy
glow of his olive-toned skin he'd gone white with shock. 'A
hard act to follow, is that it?' Learning his competition was
six feet under was not one of the greater moments in his life!
Ghosts could do no wrong.

She was so amazed at his interpretation, she didn't reply
at all. At nineteen, and working as an au pair with a delightful
couple in the South of France, she'd reacted the way most
teenage girls would have on meeting the famous brother of
her host. Raoul Fauré had been a Formula One driver as
renowned for trophy girlfriends as he was for his racing tro-
phies. His reckless skill on the circuit had brought him ad-
ulation from the public and envy from his peers.

She'd have been happy to worship from afar, but he hadn't
kept his distance; he'd told her she was the most beautiful
girl in the world and she'd believed him. His declaration of
love had been the fulfilment of all her adolescent fantasies—
what followed had been inevitable.

The next week he'd come back to the villa, only this time
he'd had a lovely young actress on his arm and in his bed.
He'd treated her with the same avuncular affection as his
brother; it was as if he genuinely didn't remember. It was
only later that she understood. At the time she'd been bewildered and miserable; her youthful idealism had suffered a
death-blow. She'd developed a convenient dose of terminal
homesickness about then and the Faurés had been sorry to

see her go, but understanding. Happily for them, they were nice people; they hadn't suspected anything.

'Chastity has a lot going for it. Sex just isn't important to me.'

'Is that a fact?' he said, not bothering to hide his scepticism.

'I just said so, didn't I?'

She realised about two seconds too late how easily her vaguely belligerent stance could have been interpreted as a challenge. It was one Benedict seemed very ready to accept. His mouth was hot and urgent—almost angry as it covered her own. The taste of him detonated an equally violent response within her; it ripped away all the elaborate barriers she'd constructed.

Her body arched as his strong arms lifted her upwards until her toes were the only things still in contact with the ground. His hard thighs ground rhythmically against her softer, more fragile frame. There was salty moisture on her skin as his dark head moved to touch, taste and torment her. Her fingers clenched tight in the dense thickness of his hair and a startled cry escaped the confines of her tight throat as her back suddenly collided with the wall.

He lifted his head at the sound. For a moment they were eye to eye and she saw the blaze of savage triumph in his dark, passion-glazed eyes. He nipped slowly at her trembling lip, letting his tongue slide into the sweet moistness within.

'You're...' she whispered hoarsely. She could hardly breathe; this sweet ache was smothering her. Hunger, viscous and warm, nibbled away at her restraints.

'I'm what? What am I, Rachel?' he persisted. As she turned her face into his shoulder he drew back fractionally; with a finger under her chin he forced her to face him. 'Tell me.' His free hand slid up her thigh, pausing momentarily only when his questing fingertips made contact with the edge of her hold-up stockings. She felt the tension that coiled in his muscles hike up a notch and heard his razor-sharp gasp.

His hand settled around the curve of her taut buttock. 'You're cruel and very...very beautiful, Ben.' He was cruel to make her want him like this...make her love... She gasped and suddenly went limp in his arms.

'This wasn't meant to happen here,' he said thickly as he stared down into her face. Her eyelashes flickered against her cheek; she looked barely conscious. But she was alive; the vigorous rise and fall of her breasts were evidence of that.

It wasn't the only thing that wasn't meant to happen, she thought in dazed disbelief as his thumb and forefinger moved up her neck before coming to rest on the pointed angle of her firm chin. His right arm was taking almost all her weight.

'Nothing's going to happen,' she said dazedly as she looked up at him. His taut features made it quite clear he was firmly in the grip of rampant desire. The evidence of this was pressed against the cradle of her hips. Trying to twist free only increased the intimate pressure. The heavy, dragging sensation had pooled low and deep in her abdomen; it was treacherously sweet.

'I've heard of denial but this is ridiculous.'

She felt the deep shudder through his body and the shivery, hot sensations in the pit of her belly responded with mindless pleasure to this evidence of his own lack of control. The dark excitement didn't respond to her wishes—at least not the wishes she consciously acknowledged.

She could see the dark pupil had swallowed up the colour of his iris completely. There was a faint sheen over his finely textured olive skin. Without thinking she reached out and ran a finger down his lean cheek. The light shadow on his skin had a fascinatingly abrasive quality. She pressed her damp finger to her lips and shivered as she tasted the faintly salty moisture.

The only flicker of movement in his entire body was the faintest stirring of his eyelashes. He didn't even appear to be breathing—this fact was confirmed when he did eventually take a deep, shuddering breath.

'Ben…'

'Hush,' he ordered huskily. His finger traced the outline of her quivering mouth before sliding inside her parted lips. The intimacy was totally devastating. 'I love your mouth. You try and make it all prim and proper and all the time it's just saying, Taste me, kiss me.'

She moaned out loud and pressed the back of her hand to her lips as he ran his tongue over the finger he'd just used to explore her mouth.

'You taste so sweet. I really like the idea of you tasting me. Would you like that?' he persisted throatily.

The erotic picture his sinful words were building made her dizzy. Her fingers tightened convulsively on the fabric of his shirt and several buttons came adrift. She felt the fabric part and even though she tried desperately not to she found herself looking downwards.

The skin over his washboard-flat belly was smooth and the tan was too dark to be attributed solely to his olive complexion. She wanted to touch him so badly, tears stung the back of her eyelids. Her body was convulsed by a feverish shudder.

'Perhaps you're right. I should just have sex with you!' The words emerged suddenly, loud and harsh. She didn't have many defences left. 'Get it all over and done with and things can go back to normal with your giant-sized ego intact—after all, no woman can refuse Ben Arden, superstud!'

Benedict lifted his head. Melting capitulation would have been nice, but Benedict wasn't a man easily discouraged. He knew a last-ditch effort when he saw one.

'There's no *perhaps* about it,' he replied huskily.

The sexy rasp combined with the suggestive heat in his eyes made her want to endorse his view. Hold on, Rachel, she told herself, harnessing her runaway tongue firmly; you're trying to defuse this situation, not ignite it!

'It's probably the simplest way to get this out of your system.' She tried to imply she was nothing but a disinterested observer—it wasn't easy.

'Is this the point where I'm supposed to be so offended by your icy detachment that I retire, my ego irretrievably bruised?' To her horror he looked amused.

'I'm just being realistic. Would you prefer I got all emotional?' Perhaps she should just confess she'd fallen in love with him—that should be more than enough to make him back off, she thought bitterly.

'Of course this strategy of yours only works if you endow me with finer feelings. If I don't recoil in disgust and say "Yes, please", you've just shot yourself in the foot,' he pointed out helpfully. 'As for a *superstud*?' He shook his head from side to side reprovingly and grimaced. 'I might just have such a high opinion of my sexual prowess that I'm confident you'll come running back for more. Or I might be callous and selfish enough to turn a blind eye to your obvious lack of interest in the whole sordid business if it means slaking my terrible lust. I really don't think you've thought this one through properly, Rachel.'

'I wouldn't actually go to bed with you!' she protested weakly.

'On the other hand,' he mused, 'if your surrender is couched in those terms you can rationalise it as being the only logical solution to a trying problem—a sacrifice for the greater good. Can it be I was doing you an injustice?' he wondered out loud. 'This removes any nasty nagging problems about how you're going to explain to yourself that you *want* me in your bed. And you just can't do that, can you, my love?'

'I'm not your love,' she choked, using up her last reserves of defiance.

'And you'll probably hate me tomorrow,' he agreed with a placidity that was contradicted by the fierce predatory glitter in his eyes.

'I hate you now.'

'That's a start.'

'Are you mad?'

'The jury's still out.'

'What are you doing?' she yelped as he swept her up into his arms. God help me, I'm enjoying playing the weak, defenceless female! she thought.

'My office has a lock and a sofa.'

The idea of a locked door gave her a completely false sense of security. 'And you have the key?' she asked, breathing hard; she'd abandoned all pretence of rejection.

'No,' he said, pressing something cold into her hand. 'You have.'

Rachel discovered the sofa was softly upholstered and the material was smooth against her naked back. The lacy bra she wore was almost but not quite transparent, and Benedict found the *almost* part incredibly arousing—at least that was what he said and his actions thereafter tended to confirm this statement.

He was kneeling beside the sofa and seeing his dark head against her as his mouth closed around the outline of her nipple where it showed dark through the flimsy fabric was incredibly erotic. She wore only the lacy pair of pants that matched the bra but he was still fully clothed, although his jacket did lie somewhere at the side of the room where he had impatiently thrown it.

Without warning he suddenly touched the skimpy triangle

of lace that barely concealed the soft, protective thatch between her legs. She jerked with shock at the intimate touch and wound one pale thigh protectively over the other.

'Don't you like that?'

She did; she liked it very much. Eyes on his, hardly able to credit her own daring, she straightened her legs.

'Yes,' she said throatily as she parted her thighs for his touch. The act of symbolic submission felt thrillingly erotic.

'It gets better,' he promised huskily. It did; the sight of his dark head bent over her, the feel of his mouth moving against the thin fabric was almost unbearably exciting. His fingers quested sensitively towards the hot core of her desire.

'Stop,' she pleaded. 'I can't bear...'

'So long as you remind me where I was...later,' he conceded. 'I think you could do with room for expansion up here,' he mused as he lifted his head. His thumb moved rhythmically against her flattened nipple; the burning sensation made her stomach muscles contract violently.

Holding his eyes, she leant slightly forward and unhooked the bra fastening. 'Is this better?'

His nostrils flared and the muscles of his throat worked as he stared at the gentle sway of her pale-pink-tipped breasts.

'It's perfect; you're perfect,' he groaned thickly. 'The first time I saw you you weren't wearing a bra under that blue dress...'

'Lilac.'

'And I could see how lovely and full and firm you were then. When you bent forward I could see just enough to...' He cleared his throat noisily. Benedict Arden blushing? That couldn't be right. 'Let's just say enough to drive me crazy. Take them off.' He hooked a thumb in the elasticated waist of her lacy pants.

'Do it for me?' she pleaded huskily.

The agonisingly slow progress of his fingers down her

thighs was almost unbearable. Free of the confinement, her hips stirred and rotated as, eyes tightly shut, she imagined him moving inside her...filling her... The choking sound he made forced her to open her eyes. The molten ferocity of his tense features convinced her he was sharing her fantasy. He looked as if he was on the brink of losing control. The idea was both exciting and appalling.

'Now come here and let me finish what I started,' she purred huskily.

He looked on with half-closed eyes as her trembling fingers slid free the remaining buttons on his shirt. The glitter she could see within the slits of his eyes made her even more clumsy. She dragged the fabric back to reveal the broad expanse of his bronzed torso; the faint sheen of moisture made his satiny skin glow. His body was built on truly magnificent lines, though his impressive musculature was not unduly bulky; he was built for flexibility, speed and grace, not just strength.

Fingers splayed, she laid her hands on him and sighed deeply. Mesmerised by the texture of his warm skin, she let her fingers move sensuously, delighting in the sharp contractions of his muscles. Her fingers slid under the waistband of his trousers and she felt a tiny quiver of uncertainty. She looked up and the expression in his eyes sent her confidence soaring.

His trousers had slipped down to his lean hips and she could see the line of hair that narrowed to a dark line that disappeared beneath the white cotton he wore underneath.

'Are you all right?'

Suddenly he sounded concerned and she lifted her head sharply, sending her thick hair fanning cloud-like about her flushed face. She tried to speak and realised that her breathing had become a series of staccato, uneven gasps. She pressed her hands to his shoulders to steady herself and tried to draw adequate breath into her lungs.

'I'm fine.' Then, in a rush of honesty, she admitted, 'I don't know my own body, not when you touch me, or I touch you. I don't recognise any of the things I'm feeling, Ben.'

She'd not acted on impulse since she was a green teenager but something compelled her to do so now. This was something she just had to share with him.

'It feels as if this is happening to someone else.'

The feverish, reckless glow in his eyes deepened. 'Perhaps I should make this more personal—more *real*.'

'There's plenty of room here.'

'Slow might not be an option once I join you there,' he confessed, looking at the narrow space she patted with sultry invitation.

'It's a risk I'm willing to take.'

'Comfortable?' he asked as he cleverly insinuated his body under hers.

'Not really the word I'd use,' she gasped, finding herself sitting astride him. His back was against the arm of the sofa and they were eye to eye.

Then she wasn't using any words at all because he was guiding her nipple into his mouth. The slow, sumptuous friction of his tongue and lips was agonisingly arousing.

Rachel gave a deep moan and her body jerked violently before sagging against him. One of his hands rested in the small of her back and the other sank into her hair. The sweeping motion as his fingers sank into the luxuriant growth pulled her head backwards, leaving her neck sinews taut. His mouth moved upwards to the irresistible temptation of the graceful curve, leaving a trail of burning kisses. The warm scent rising from his skin made her body ache almost as much as his expert touch. *Expert.*

'What's wrong?' he asked, picking up on her sudden mental withdrawal almost instantaneously. His breath was hot against her cheek as his tongue moved in lazy, teasing circles over the ultra-sensitive skin beside her ear.

Chin resting against his shoulder, her body leaning bone-lessly against him, she slid her arms tightly around his middle, pulling tightly as if the contact would ease the sudden flurry of insecurities.

'I'm not exactly experienced…I haven't done this for…' Before she hadn't really been a participant at all. Her contribution had been compliance. Ben wanted more than that. What if she disappointed him? 'My body isn't perfect…I've had a child.'

'Do you think I'm asking for perfection?' He sounded angry and when he forced her chin up he looked it, too. His dark eyes were filled with a resentment she didn't quite understand. 'Do you think making love can be rated on a scale of one to ten? There hasn't been a measurement invented that can accurately describe the way it feels to touch your skin.'

'Try,' she said, intoxicated and immensely relieved by the sincerity of his words. 'Try and tell me?'

'It's easier if I show you.' He firmly guided her hand downwards to the painfully congested area between his thighs. His response to her light touch made her gasp and smile with greedy, erotic satisfaction. Lips parted slightly, she lifted her passion-glazed gaze to his face.

'This thing limits our options.' He banged his head against the upholstered arm before sliding dramatically downwards and pulling her with him. 'It's either you up there and me down here, or me up here—' her soft shriek was smothered by the erotic imprint of his marauding mouth '—and you down there. The choice is yours.'

'I'm easy.'

Deep laughter vibrated in his chest. 'Would that were true. What are you…?' He inclined his head to see her drag his already loosened trousers and his shorts over his hips. She felt the hot, hard tip of his arousal nudge against her belly and fought hard to retain control. The gap between consciousness and dark oblivion was dangerously close.

'I'm showing initiative,' she said, lifting her head just close enough for the tip of her tongue to lap back and forward over the dark stud of one male nipple. She reached up and pulled his shirt, which flapped around them, a couple of inches down over the flexed muscles of his shoulders. The fabric didn't give and the constriction caused him to collapse down on his elbows.

'I'll squash you,' he warned hoarsely.

'I like being squashed by you,' she reassured him. She hooked her legs up and around his waist, locking her ankles firmly over his back.

'Rachel!' he rumbled in warning, the contorted expression on his face reflecting the strain he was under. He slid between her thighs because there was nowhere else for him to go. 'I can't move.'

'You can. You can move exactly where I want you to go.'

'I've never made love with my shoes on. My clothes.'

'Don't worry, we can work around them.' Only one thing could satisfy her now.

'Work around!' A hoarse laugh emerged from his dry throat. 'You're a very bad girl, Rachel,' he said thickly. 'You mean I'm on top, but you're in charge?'

'Now you come to mention it...' The air was expelled from her lungs in one long sigh as he slid firmly into her body. All thoughts of domination and control vanished at the precise moment her body expanded to accommodate his pulsing masculinity.

'You're—' She gasped, sliding her arms beneath his shirt to grip the slick, warm flesh of his back.

'I'm what?' he asked thickly, his voice almost unrecognisable. Rachel was beyond words; she only wanted to absorb him, feel him move within her.

He couldn't resist her pleas and any restraint he had vanished under the onslaught of her inarticulate entreaties and encouragements. He could no longer control the aggression of his thrusts as he gave her what she asked for—all of him.

'Oh, God, I didn't use a condom!'

As post-coital sweet nothings went this really ruined the mood.

'Don't worry, it's not a fertile time of my cycle.' If the sofa had come supplied with sheets she'd have used them to cover her vulnerability. And a whole lot more than her vulnerability was showing just now! She edged as far away from his sweat-covered body as possible.

'That's not the point.'

'It isn't?' She wanted so badly to touch him. Would it be so bad? she wondered wistfully.

'I wouldn't want you to think I'm normally reckless.'

'Relax, I don't.'

'Next time—'

'There won't be a next time.'

She felt the sofa groan as he raised himself on one elbow. Under the circumstances it was impossible to avoid his eyes. 'Oh?'

His eyes ran slowly over her slim body, still flushed from their strenuous lovemaking.

'I'm not blaming you.'

'That's good of you.' The droll smile that lifted one corner of his mouth wasn't reflected in his eyes.

'But it can't happen again.'

'If you're willing to give me ten minutes and some encouragement I think you'll find it can.'

The heat tore through her body as her imagination responded to the vivid images conjured up by his words. 'I need to go home.'

'Let me guess, I'm not the sort of man you want to take home to Charlie.' He didn't look or sound amused.

'I don't want to raise her expectations, Ben. She's fond of you...'

'And her mother?'

'You're a very attractive man.'

'I can hear a "but" in your voice.'

'Don't be like this,' she begged unevenly. 'It's not as if you're planning to share your life with me, is it? We've nothing whatever in common and I've not the mental attitude that makes a happy harem member.' She dredged the light laughter up from somewhere when he didn't respond with a firm proclamation that she was the one and only girl for him— she hadn't really expected him to.

'It's better for everyone concerned if we return things to a professional basis. I'd like to get dressed now.' It was probably too late even now to save herself from all the classic symptoms of addiction, but she had to make a token effort to escape.

'At this point am I supposed to avert my eyes while you make yourself decent? Sorry, Rachel, I like looking at you nude. Surely you don't begrudge a man something to remember when we're back to a professional basis?'

'Do you always make situations like this so awkward?'

'It may surprise you, Rachel, but even with my varied, much documented love life I've never found myself in this situation before. I wasn't expecting slavish adoration...'

'No?' The sooner that little time bomb was skirted the better! 'Just applause possibly? I think you're just peeved because the women you date wait for *you* to call it a day.' Anticipating the fact that he was about to get a lot more physical, she slid sinuously off the sofa and landed on her bottom.

He leaned over the edge and she reached for her discarded shirt, pulling it protectively over her breasts.

'Date! What date? You did promise me dinner when I took you to the hospital… I think you'd like me better if your first impressions had been right and I was some penniless bum on the prowl. You were falling over yourself to dole out the tea and sympathy then. The fact I've got anything to offer you is obviously a big turn-off! Does a relationship on equal terms scare you that much?'

Equal? Was he serious? She dreamt about equal. She sat on her heels and jerkily shoved her arms into the shirt. 'Offer me! When did you ever offer me anything?'

'There doesn't seem much point when you throw every gesture back in my face.'

'Fine! If you want dinner, I'll buy you dinner, and you can bring me flowers to say thank you. I promise I won't throw them back in your face. It's not that I didn't enjoy…' she began awkwardly.

'I know that.' He watched as she unsuccessfully tried to tug the shirt over her hips and his anger seemed to subside. He tugged up his trousers but didn't bother fastening the belt. 'When?' She looked at him blankly, worried by the rather calculating expression on his face. 'Dinner,' he reminded her.

'What? Oh, tomorrow if you like.'

'Good girl; get it over with as soon as possible. I bet you always ate your greens before the good bits. Good strategy. Are you looking for these?' Swinging his legs to the floor, he held out a pair of lacy pants at arm's length.

She lunged automatically and he withdrew his hand. 'That was tomorrow, was it? Eight o'clock?'

'Yes, yes!' she replied as he dangled the scrap of material

just out of her reach. She gave a sigh of relief as he released his grip.

'Our first date,' he said, raising an invisible glass to his lips. 'I'll return this at a later date,' he added, audaciously tucking her bra into his pocket. 'You look much better without it. I'll let you put it on so that I can have the pleasure of taking it off.'

'Our only date,' she choked defiantly.

CHAPTER SIX

'I NEED to go to the ladies' room.' Charlie laid her napkin to one side. 'Don't let them take that away,' she added, frowning suspiciously at one of the zealous waiters. 'I haven't finished yet.'

'It continually amazes me how much you can pack away,' Rachel said, getting to her feet.

'I'm not a *baby*. I'm quite capable of going on my own.'

'Pardon me…' Rachel kept her expression grave, to avoid giving any impression that she was laughing. A ten-year-old's pride was a delicate thing.

'Besides, you'll *have* to talk to Ben if I'm not here.'

And look who's laughing now, Rachel thought, staring after her daughter's retreating back.

'Out of the mouths of babes…' Benedict drawled, leaning back in his seat and enjoying the expression of discomfiture that spread across Rachel's face.

'Are you suggesting I brought Charlie along as a…a…?'

'Shield? Perish the thought.' His dark brows lifted in sardonic assurance. 'I'm sure it just slipped your mind when you issued the invitation to mention that we weren't going to be alone.'

'I owed you dinner…this is dinner.' Even if he'd seen through her somewhat transparent ruse he might have tactfully not said so.

'Was I complaining?' He grinned and reached across the table and took hold of her hand. 'Relax,' he advised as she stiffened. 'I'm having a great time. Charlie's great.' He shrugged and his ironic smile deepened. 'She hogs the conversation, but the same has been said of me. We have a surprising amount in common, you know; I was a so-called "gifted" child too. I've been through the whole hothouse thing.'

That explained the rapport. 'What hothouse thing?' she asked, ultra-sensitive to implied criticism.

'You know, skipping the bud stage and going straight into full bloom. That's the system these schools who cater for the *crème de la crème* specialise in.' He cast a knowledgeable glance at the militant light that had entered her eyes. 'And lower those prickles, darling; I don't want to fight.'

'You've got a funny way of showing it.' She had enough insecurities about her decision over Charlie's education without him making her feel even less sure about her move to the city.

'I know how it must be; on one hand you don't want to be a pushy mother, on the other you don't want to stifle her potential. It's a classic no-win situation so relax and play it by ear. Right now,' he confided, 'there's only one thing I want to ask you about Charlie. What time will she be safely in bed?'

Rachel recognised a leading question when she heard one. 'On weekends her bedtime's flexible.'

'You could always prop her up in the corner if she dozes off.' His sarcasm stung.

She snatched her hand away. His thumb had been inscribing slow, sensuous circles over the palm of her hand; her nerve-endings were jangling and she found it impossible to concentrate on anything above the clamour.

How, she pondered bleakly, was it possible for this man to do more damage to her nervous system with such an innocuous caress than anyone else could manage with a full-scale seduction?

'You'll be gone long before then,' she said pointedly.

'Are you trying to tell me something, Rachel? It couldn't be you're scared of being alone with me, could it?'

Rachel gritted her teeth and displayed them in a brilliant smile. His smug confidence really got under her skin—especially as she had a sinking feeling it could well be justified.

'I am alone with you and see—' she held out her hand for his inspection '—not even a tremor.'

'Steady as a rock,' he agreed admiringly, 'but very much prettier.' He bent forward and touched his lips to the back of her extended hand.

She gasped; she couldn't help it; the neat electricity made her toes curl tightly in her elegant high heels. Benedict raised his dark head slowly and she pulled her hand back, nursing it protectively in her lap—not even the best will in the world could have kept the tremors at bay now.

'There are things I need to say to you that are better said in private, Rachel.'

'I don't think I want to hear them,' she confessed, too flustered to compose a less truthful reply.

'Why?'

Through the protective shield of her lashes she watched him fill up her glass with wine which she had no intention of consuming—she needed all her wits about her tonight.

'You're going away.'

Too late for me, she thought grimly as she hung grittily onto what composure she had left. She could see it might be nice for him to have some blatantly besotted idiot to while away the time with before he packed his bags and moved to the other side of the world, but she wasn't going to be that idiot.

'And does that bother you?' The dark eyes were fixed with unnerving intensity on her face.

'If you're waiting for me to say I'll be devastated, don't hold your breath,' she returned calmly.

'I really like that in you.'

'Like what?'

'You're a fighter, a real scrapper.' Elbows on the table, he rested his chin in his hands and allowed his eyes to wander admiringly over her flushed face. 'Only you ought to accept there are some things you just can't fight.'

'Really?' she said, compressing her lips and suppressing the urge to run—well, she was still sitting anyhow.

'You were about to say, Such as? Only you thought better of it.'

'Now you're a mind-reader too.'

'Last night we both seemed to be doing a lot of that.' The slow, husky drawl, only a notch above a whisper, had a resonance that vibrated through her tense body. She couldn't tear her eyes from the lips that had formed the words and once she started looking the remembering was inevitable. She remembered how those lips, applied in various imaginative ways, had reduced her to a... She shook her head to clear the images that flooded through her disorientated mind.

'I thought we'd agreed that that was a one-off thing,' she said harshly.

'I didn't agree to anything; you agreed for us both,' he reminded her. 'I didn't think you were the sort of girl who went in for one-night stands, Rachel?'

'Neither did I,' she admitted with a flash of honesty. She suspected he knew as well as she did that that put her in a situation where she had to say no; one night would no longer be an appropriate description.

'Would it make a difference if I wasn't going away?'

The sly question threw her shaky balance completely for six. 'Naturally I'm flattered you haven't got bored with me just yet. But...don't you think you should get a bit of practice with normal relationships before you contemplate the long-distance variety?' She and Benedict didn't want the same things from relationships. She knew what she wanted, but it wasn't on offer.

'And if I wasn't leaving would you offer to repair that gap in my education?'

'My spare time's pretty full at present.' The linen napkin was crushed beyond salvation in her fingers. 'I don't think you're ready for the sort of...'

'Commitment.' He pounced almost eagerly on the opening in her faltering explanation.

Rachel had already heard his opinion on longevity and permanence; she didn't want to offer him the opportunity to rub salt in the wound. She didn't want to join the legion of women who pursued him.

'Here's Charlie...'

The fleeting expression of seething frustration that flickered through Benedict's eyes made it quite clear that the levity in his manner had been masking deeper, more urgent emotions. Only Rachel didn't see it because her attention was riveted on the man beside her daughter. Good God, he was talking to her.

'Rachel?'

Concern replaced frustration as she continued to stare beyond him. She looked, he thought, as though she'd seen a ghost. He automatically turned to see what was causing her such alarm.

It looked innocuous enough; Charlie was handing an empty glass to a tall guy who was patting his damp shirt-front. He looked to be taking the incident in his stride. The Italian proprietor's laid-back attitude to children had obviously rubbed off on some of the patrons too.

Rachel saw his body freeze as Charlie straightened up. He said something quickly and she saw Charlie nod towards their table. Her heart thudded as they moved closer. It was a long time since she'd wondered if this situation would ever arise. The chances of her meeting one of the Faurés were remote, but remote had happened.

'Hello, Rachel.'

'Christophe, this is a surprise,' she said huskily.

'For me too,' he said heavily.

The guy had one of those French accents females found attractive. Benedict tried not to hold the accent against him; after all, he was an open-minded sort of guy. However, despite his open-minded attitude he found he couldn't stretch to a smile when the older man glanced in his direction.

'You are married, Rachel?'

'No, no…this is Benedict Arden. Ben, this is Christophe Fauré.'

'And I have met Charlie.'

It was then, as he smiled down at the child, that it finally clicked: the eyes. Charlie had his eyes! That was why he'd looked familiar. No wonder Rachel had looked as if she was seeing a ghost; she *was* seeing a ghost. Benedict had felt a similar sensation when a cricket ball had hit his unprotected adolescent manhood when he was thirteen.

'Are you in London alone?' This was a nightmare, Rachel decided; a waking nightmare. Christophe knew; of course he knew. He was seeing his brother as he looked at Charlie. She didn't have the faintest idea what his reaction would be.

'Annabel stayed at home. She has an exhibition next month. My wife,' he said, glancing politely at Benedict. 'She is an artist.'

'So you're married.' The hostility would have been hard to miss.

'Yes.'

'A question occurs to me.' This was Benedict at his most bland and Rachel, who hadn't thought things could get much worse, thought she might be sick. 'Were you married when you and Rachel last…met?'

'I was.'

'And when might that have been?'

'*Ben!*' She frowned reprovingly at him. He was behaving like a heavy parent, for heaven's sake! Or a jealous lover... She pushed this notion and the accompanying spurt of dangerous gratification firmly away.

'Eleven years ago.' Christophe's eyes repeatedly strayed to Charlie as he went on, 'Your mother was our au pair, Charlie. She kept house for us for a while. She was not very much older than you really.'

God, what was he going to say next? she wondered with alarm. She could almost hear the questions forming in Charlie's mind. If Charlie was going to hear the story she was going to hear it from her mother's lips.

'Dance with me,' she said, urgency lending her inspiration. Christophe looked startled. '*Please*, Christophe?' Her smile was all teeth and terror. She had to get him away from Charlie.

'I'd be delighted.'

'Sorry,' she said a few minutes later as she trod on his toes for the second time.

'She is Raoul's of course,' he said, breaking the silence.

Silently Rachel nodded.

'He was my brother and I loved him but he was a selfish....'

Rachel's French was good enough to translate the unflattering epithet accurately.

'And I was a silly girl,' she added, not disagreeing with his harsh assessment of his dead brother's character.

'Did he know?'

'No.'

'That's something, I suppose. I'd like to think it would have made a difference if he had...' He left his doubts unspoken. 'You were living under our roof,' he continued in a severe voice. 'Our responsibility. I should have guessed and been more vigilant; I knew how Raoul was—without honour.' His lips twisted in disgust. 'Charlie is my niece—my blood; I could have helped. I hope you didn't tar us with the same brush as Raoul. I would understand if you did.'

'No, of course not; you and Annabel were very kind to me. I was ashamed, frightened. I didn't want anyone to know I'd been so stupid. Later, when I heard about the crash, I thought about letting you know, but I thought you might think I was after... Well, it would have looked pretty suspicions: I pop up complete with child when Raoul is no longer there to deny or confirm my story.'

'Charlie's eyes are all the proof you needed,' he said, his frown deepening. 'My family have done you harm, Rachel. Helping you would have been a privilege, not just a duty.'

Rachel's throat was suddenly choked with emotion at the sincerity in this man's voice. It was amazing that two brothers could be so dissimilar, she reflected sadly.

'And this man who looks at me with murder in his eyes—what is he to you?'

'Benedict! He wouldn't...' There was only one other couple on the dance floor and she had an unobstructed view of their table. She saw Benedict's face and changed her mind—it looked distinctly possible that he would! There was nothing sophisticated about his expression—it was one of crude, violent disapproval.

'Perhaps he doesn't like you dancing with other men.'

'It's none of his business who I dance with,' she responded, her mouth settling into a combative line. He expected her to get her mind around his colourful past; how perverse could you get? Even if he had assumed that Christophe was her former lover—and from his confrontational attitude that seemed very likely—he had no right to come over all possessive.

A sceptical expression stirred in Christophe's eyes, but he maintained a diplomatic silence. 'I would like to make amends—too late, I know. Don't!' he said, pressing a finger to her lips, which were parted to refuse. 'The request is self-ish also. Annabel and I couldn't have children.' Behind the stoical acceptance Rachel had a glimpse of pain and her tender heart ached.

'There is no young blood in our family and the sound of a child's voice would bring us all delight. Don't deny my mother her only grandchild, Rachel. You and Charlie could visit us in France; we could all get to know one another.'

'Charlie and I don't have any family either.' She couldn't believe it was this simple! Suddenly there was a grand-mother, a whole family Charlie had never met. Not in her wildest dreams had she pictured such ready acceptance.

Christophe sighed. 'Thank you, Rachel,' he said simply. 'Now you'd better tell me your address before I return you to your young man.'

'He's not mine '

'I think he might dispute that,' came the dry reply.

'I want *Ben* to say goodnight.' Charlie wielded her dripping toothbrush like a conductor's baton and her attitude was just as imperious.

It's nice to be wanted, Rachel thought as she watched Ben sketch a courtly bow. 'Your wish, my lady, is my command,' he said solemnly.

She bent to receive her daughter's kiss, worry behind her strained smile. It would be kinder to Charlie if she severed her connections with Benedict Arden cleanly. She'd never seen Charlie take such a shine to anyone before. It would be selfish and weak to listen to the insidious voice in her head that told her to forget her pride and enjoy what little time they had together. Deep down she had no doubt that had she been single that would have been exactly what she would be doing now—and to hell with the consequences!

When Benedict reappeared a few moments later the careful words of her 'it was nice while it lasted' speech fragmented. Looking at him made her feel weak and irresolute.

'Ben, I...er...that is...' She bit her lip and tried to reassemble her thoughts. The emptiness inside hurt now. It had always been there, but it was only since Benedict had got a handhold in her life that she'd recognised it for what it was— loneliness. He was going to go away anyway; she might as well feel the pain now as later.

'He didn't know about Charlie, did he?'

There was no question in her mind concerning the identity of the 'he' he referred to. The abrupt, expressionless accusation had robbed her of what little brain function she had left. He knew...how?

'No,' she heard herself confess. 'I never expected to see him again. He and his wife...'

'Oh, yes, the wife.'

She hardly noticed the sneer in his voice. Perhaps, she reflected, it would help sort things out in her own mind if she discussed the situation with someone. And Ben seemed to know so...

'They can't have any children so Christophe—'

'I don't believe this!'

She watched in confusion as Benedict ground his balled fist into the palm of his other hand. 'Why would he lie? He's no reason—'

'No reason!' he yelled. 'That's the truth, isn't it? You're obviously prepared to take everything he says at face value. One word from *him* and you're prepared to forgive and forget. Haven't you learnt anything from the past?' he asked incredulously. His dark eyes moved angrily over her face.

'It wasn't Christophe's fault,' she protested. She couldn't blame the man for his brother's misdeeds.

Benedict sucked in his breath and his slanted cheekbones jutted even harder against the taut flesh of his face. Everything about him seemed tight; the explosive quality in him was tangible.

'In my book,' he ground out, 'a man—an *older, married* man—who seduces a young girl—scarcely more than a schoolgirl—who is living under his own roof is...' He tilted his chin to one side as if considering the problem. '*Responsible,*' he drawled, his eyes shooting smoky fire. 'I'd say that about covers it. He's a lot of other things too,' he lashed from between clenched teeth. 'But I won't offend your delicate sensibilities by listing them. Only your feelings aren't too delicate where he is concerned, are they? The bastard was all over you.

'How are you going to explain her father's miraculous resurrection to Charlie? He gets a ready-made family—convenient, to comfort him in his declining years. And they're not too far away,' he added viciously. 'You really do have a thing about older men, don't you? You've got to admire the man,' he drawled, betraying no sign of that particular emotion. 'He really does seize the opportunity.'

Too late she realised that Christophe hadn't been the only one to notice the family resemblance. Whilst Christophe didn't resemble Raoul in any other way they did share the same distinctive blue eyes—Charlie's eyes. She'd been so distracted by his unexpected appearance, she hadn't realised that Ben had seemed unusually withdrawn and quiet on the way home. All the signs had been there—how could she have been so blind?

'Ben,' she said urgently.

'I never had you pegged as gullible, Rachel.' Obviously listening wasn't high on his list of priorities. He had a lot to say, though, and the delay in getting it out of his system hadn't helped any. 'God, woman, you're not a green nine-teen-year-old now. What is it about this guy that sends your judgement haywire? You've been suspicious enough of *me*. You continually endow my most innocent action with sinister motives.' Jaw taut, he shook his head disbelievingly. 'I suppose if he asks you to go to France with him...'

'He already has.' She knew now what she had to do.

It might break her heart, but using his misinterpretation of the situation might be the simplest—no, *only* way she was going to get Benedict Arden out of her life, and get him out for Charlie's sake she must. Her admission had stopped him dead; it had hurt too, she could see that. Even if his pain could be attributed solely to hurt pride it still made her want to explain.

'He doesn't waste much time,' he said slowly, breaking the stunned silence that had followed her words. 'And you said— No, don't bother telling me; it's obvious what you said.' He picked his jacket up from the back of the sofa and flung it over his shoulder. 'You may think you're mistress material, Rachel, but you're not.'

Suddenly she couldn't bear to let him go away thinking... 'Ben,' she said urgently, 'it's not the way it seems.'

'Men like that don't change, Rachel. Women just like to think they're the one who will break the pattern.'

His words stopped her in her tracks. 'You should know,' she agreed. Could he really not see the irony of his warning?

'Sure, I've seduced women and been seduced in my turn, but I've *never* destroyed anyone—I'm not a user. He'll break your heart, Rachel—he's done it before—and who's going to pick up the pieces?'

'Not you; you won't be here.' You're the one breaking my heart, you stupid, *stupid* man, she wanted to scream.

'But I'm here now.' A thoughtful expression she didn't

trust entered his eyes. The way his glance moved suggestively over her body was an insult. Insults didn't usually have
this effect on her body, though. His smile was hatefully
knowing as she raised her crossed arms to cover her tingling
breasts which were only covered by a thin layer of silk. 'He's
not.'

'I wish you weren't,' she responded with feeling.

'You weren't so anxious to get rid of me before the blast
from the past reappeared.'

'You make it sound as though I laid down the red carpet.
The way I recall it you've conned your way in here each and
every time. Never use the truth when a lie will get you where
you want to be,' she sneered.

It hit her forcibly that she'd just given a fairly accurate
description of her own behaviour in enforcing Ben's belief
that Christophe was Charlie's father. If he wondered why she
suddenly subsided, blushing guiltily, he didn't ask.

'Where I want to be,' he mused slowly.

Oh, help! Her ribs didn't feel substantial enough to cage
the wild tattoo of her heart. His eyes had turned her resistance
to molten desire.

'I want…' he said, catching his breath sharply as she nervously touched the tip of her tongue to her dry lips. 'I want
to be feeling your bare breasts against my chest and I want
to be hearing your voice begging…pleading. I want to be
inside you, Rachel. Will the truth get me where I want to be
this time?'

'You can't talk to me like that,' she gasped. 'It's…it's
offensive.'

'It's the truth, and you're not offended, Rachel. You're
aroused.'

The achingly erotic words were swirling around in her
head, gathering impetus rather than losing impact as, eyes

wide and fearful, pink lips slightly parted, she stared helplessly back at him.

'So am I.'

Rachel willed her eyes not to drop from his face. She could
fell the faint beading of perspiration break out over her upper
lip. The conflicting emotions were tearing her to pieces.

'I'll take your word for it,' she managed hoarsely. I'll
show him I can cope with sexual innuendo—not that there
had been much innuendo about his comments, she thought
ruefully. Advances didn't get much more direct!

'Not just when I'm with you—when I see you. Just thinking about you is enough.' He gave a sudden hard laugh. 'And
I think about you a lot, Rachel. It conjures up a picture of
adolescent excess to bring a smile of superiority to your
lovely lips. You're not smiling. Doesn't it make you feel
powerful?'

Powerful! That was the last thing she felt. She'd never felt
so helpless in her life. She felt weak, needy, out of control
and likely to fall victim to spontaneous combustion any second. Tiny black specks began to dance before her glazed
eyes. It took an immense effort to make the buzzing in her
ears diminish to a dull roar.

'Perhaps, Rachel...' His tone had dropped to a husky, intimate drawl. The jacket he'd unceremoniously dropped was
trampled underfoot as he covered the space between them.
She had a whimsical image of him trampling all over her
will-power with his handmade size elevens. Rejection wasn't
what he read in her face or body and it showed in his self-
assurance.

'Perhaps my gross, offensive words make you feel hot
and...' He drew a sharp, shuddering breath that involved all
the muscles of his impressive chest. 'I like to think of your
body warm and moist...ready for me.' Hands resting on her
shoulders, his fingers stroked her neck.

'It is.' Whatever residual defences she'd had had crumbled at the first rasp of his erotic confessions.

He reached for her then, pulling her against him with a hungry desperation. His mouth was greedy and hot as his tongue made a slow, lascivious meal of the inner recesses of her parted lips.

'Rachel…Rachel.' He was mumbling her name in between open-mouthed kisses and tantalising soft bites. His hands moved jerkily over her body. One arm swept her closer as it tightened around her slender waist until her weight was almost wholly supported by the strength of his braced legs.

She clung, she whimpered as their embrace grew more frenzied and urgent. The sensual maelstrom carried her along until she had no thought in her head that didn't involve the taste and texture of the man who held her.

'Where?' he said, one arm half out of the shirt she had unbuttoned. 'Where is your room?' he panted.

'Over there.' She gestured vaguely behind her and her arm was still elegantly curved in a graceful arc over her head as he picked her up. Head back, her body curved with sinuous grace, she felt the dragging weight of her hair as it obeyed gravity.

'I don't have a double bed,' she commented, looking up at him with sultry speculation from her narrow single bed. What would he do next…? Each individual nerve fibre in her body was tensed in pleasurable anticipation.

'We'll cope,' he said confidently, straddling her over his knee. 'This is pretty; I like this.' His fingers worked at slipping the rouleau loops that held her pale blue camisole together. He didn't remove it; he just pushed aside the fabric to reveal the peaks of her engorged breasts. 'But not as pretty as these.' He laid his hands at either side of her breasts and examined his prize with enraptured eyes.

Rachel groaned in languid ecstasy as his clever tongue set

about paying homage to these twin symbols of her femininity. Her head fell forward, her chin angled against the top of
his bent head. She let her hands slide, palms flat, from his
shoulders down the marvellous sculpted perfection of his
back. The action brought her up on her knees. Face still bur-
ied between her breasts, Benedict growled and slid his hands
under her raised buttocks and a sharp jerk brought her hard
against the pulsing evidence of his arousal.

His hands still cradled her hips as he fell backwards on
the narrow mattress. Rachel found herself astride his half-
naked body. 'Take my clothes off, Rachel; undress me,' he
commanded throatily. He reached up and took the weight of
her breasts in the palms of his hands. He gave a deep grunt
of male satisfaction.

His dark hands against her pale skin—skin that had ac-
quired an opalescent sheen in the semi-darkness—was incredibly arousing. The way his thumbs moved softly over the
hard peaks made her breath escape from her lungs in one
silent whoosh. He caught her hands in his.

'Let me show you how. Shall I show you how, Rachel?'

Her fingers turned within his light grasp and she raised
one hand to her lips. His fingers flexed until the bones
cracked as, open-mouthed, she kissed the slightly calloused
palm of his hand. Her tongue traced a delicate damp pattern
against his flesh.

'I'd like that. Teach me, Ben.'

'You've worked out a nice line in torture all by yourself,
lover,' he groaned.

'Don't you like it?' *Lover*—it sounded good, she decided
dreamily. Why shouldn't she be his lover? Was it asking too
much to have this time with him—the man she loved?

A laugh rumbled in his chest at the husky note of sulky
pique but his eyes were fierce. 'You seem to know what I
like, Rachel.'

'It's easier if you tell me.' She hooked one finger into the curling hair that was sprinkled over his chest and belly and bent closer to lap tentatively at his flat masculine nipple. He gasped hard and sucked in his belly, emphasising the solid slabs of muscle.

'That's good,' he breathed thickly, catching hold of the back of her head and urging her back down. 'We could start there.' He closed his eyes as the lash of her delicate tongue began once more. Periodically she raised her head to peep with sultry satisfaction at the tense, almost pained expression that contorted his features.

'I like this,' she sighed, tucking her damp hair behind her ears and throwing him another hot, hungry look.

'Let's find out what else you like.' Abruptly he tipped her pliant body backwards and Rachel found herself flat on her back with him kneeling over her.

'I didn't finish,' she said, tugging at the buckle of his leather belt.

'Two sets of hands make light work,' he said. He yanked his trousers down his legs and kicked them clear.

The excitement moved low in her belly at the sight of his arousal. The pain was sharp, the emotions deep and suffocating. The weight of hot, unshed tears stung her eyes. Nobody but Ben could ever make her feel like this—it wasn't possible.

'I'm glad.'

His words startled her; she hadn't been conscious of speaking. 'Shall I touch...?' She reached out and paused, suddenly not quite the sultry temptress she'd been playing.

'Yes—oh, yes!'

The red sparks that danced before her eyes seemed visible evidence of the sexual energy that crackled around them. The husky encouragement was all she needed to soothe the flurry of uncertainty. She was now sure that what she wanted to do was what he wanted too.

The room was filled with sharp gasps and hoarse groans as he moved against her hand until the moment came when his hand covered her own. She made a sound of protest.

'I'm a marathon man myself; I like to appreciate the journey. But if you keep that up...'

'You're saving yourself for a sprint finish?' she suggested with an impish grin.

'Only if you behave, you little witch,' he said, responding to her teasing with a mock growl. He pinned her arms to her sides. She squirmed, not from any desire to escape but because it felt good to have his heavy body pressing against her.

'Do you really want me to behave?' she asked, panting from the exertions of their mock combat. His breath stirred the downy hair on her cheek; he smelt distinctively of Ben.

'Naturally—I want you to behave naturally, Rachel.'

She could do that, she thought happily; at least, she could with Ben. He obeyed the implicit plea in her passion-saturated eyes and kissed her.

Rachel wasn't conscious of shedding her remaining clothes but it wasn't very long before his elegant, sensitive fingers were moving unimpeded over her smooth flesh. His clever fingers roused her past and beyond thought; she was all feeling and sensation. The primitive regression was complete and now she needed him—needed him badly to finish what he'd started.

'Yes...yes...yes!' she cried as he slid into her. Feeling her body adapt and stretch to accept him was a breathless, marvellous sensation, and when he began to move she wrapped her legs around him and let everything happen. It did happen perfectly.

Sleepy and languid in the aftermath, she couldn't feel regret. She burrowed like a kitten against him. Tiny aftershocks still tightened the muscles in her pelvis but she hadn't forgotten the moment of release; she never would.

'I wasn't going to do this again,' she murmured sleepily.

'Is that what you thought?' he replied indulgently.

'I don't say goodbye to everyone like this, you know.' A faint whimsical smile curved her lips. Her languid state of mind didn't register the sudden tension in the arms of the man who held her.

'Goodbye?' Rachel didn't hear his harsh question; she'd finally released her tenacious grip on consciousness.

'I think it's best if you leave now.'

The sleepy look on Ben's face made him look younger than his thirty-four years. The impulse to wrap her arms around him was strong. It would have felt good to have him wake up next to her. His dark head had been comfortably settled against the slope of her breasts before she had stealthily slipped from the warm bed.

Benedict dragged his fingers through his tousled dark hair and the sheet slid down to reveal his hair-roughened chest and flat belly.

'You're saying basically "Here's your pants; get lost"?' He jackknifed into a sitting position and from his alert expression his brain was no longer burdened by fatigue—it was firing on all cylinders.

'I'm saying it would be better if you left before Charlie wakes up. She'll be confused...'

'That'll make two of us.'

He didn't look confused; he looked angry. She'd hoped he wouldn't react like this.

'Be reasonable. I'm the one who'll have to field awkward questions,' she reminded him tensely.

'Are you sure it's the thought of Charlie's questions that's got you running scared, Rachel? Wouldn't it be more honest to say it's your own questions you're prepared to go to any lengths to avoid?' He flung back the quilt and swung his long legs over the side of the bed. The sight made her sensitive stomach muscles go into spasm.

Why don't you go ahead and drool? she asked herself angrily as she tore her glance from the sight of his athletically sculpted thighs.

'It's a perfectly legitimate request,' she said, tightening the sash on her smoky blue floor-length gown. He got up and walked across the room. There was no hint of self-consciousness in his graceful stride. He was as close to perfection as it came, she thought, watching him with covetous eyes.

'It makes it pretty clear that you're ashamed of last night.'

'Last night was just a…a…'

'The definitive term escapes you, does it?'

She glared resentfully at him. He appeared to get some savage satisfaction from seeing her floundering helplessly. 'I'm just being practical,' she insisted.

'Does the idea of sex full stop bother you, or is it just sex with me that becomes sordid and tacky in the cold light of day?'

There was a depth of anger and disillusionment she hadn't expected in his expression. She stifled the flicker of uncertainty before gritting her teeth and continuing in a patronising, amused tone, 'Don't worry, this is no reflection on your masculinity. I'll go on record as saying you're a fantastic lover.' She smiled and lifted her shoulders in a tiny gesture intended to reflect on the fragile ego of the male.

He stepped into his white cotton boxers and his brows drew together in a hard line of displeasure. 'Did I measure up to your idealised memories of your first love? Fantasies are so much neater, don't you find? There's no body to get rid of in the morning.' He smiled unpleasantly at her. 'Thank you,' he added as she passed him the errant sock which had been eluding him.

He only raised a brow when she jerked her hand away before their fingers touched, but it was enough to make her flush self-consciously. If he had any idea of how much she feared a simple contact like that and why, she'd die of sheer humiliation.

'Unlike you I don't consider sex a leisure sport. I'm sure some people can be satisfied...'

'I thought you were. You screamed something to that effect, as I recall.'

'Must you be crude and vulgar?' she asked, her cheeks ablaze. 'I'm trying to say I can't justify sex without love.'

'Well, you're not doing a very good job of it. Practical's a good line,' he mused. 'You stick to that, darling,' he advised. 'Anyone can say "I love you".'

'I don't.'

'I'd noticed,' he said with a savage inflection. 'I'm sure your Gallic charmer did—bilingually, probably—and look where that got you. At the end of the day actions speak louder than words; words are ten-a-penny.'

'When you say them I'm sure that's true.'

'You mean I wouldn't have been welcomed back to bed if I'd sworn undying love?' he asked incredulously. He gave a strange twisted smile as though the black humour in his eyes was aimed at himself.

'I'm not *that* gullible.' To hear him joking about something about which she'd nursed improbable fantasies cut deep.

'Just as well I didn't waste my breath, then, isn't it? It obviously hasn't occurred to you, but if you were a man kicking his partner out with indecent haste at five a.m. it would be a different story.'

'I don't believe this! Are you implying *I'm* using *you*?'
She gasped incredulously at this novel interpretation of the
situation.

'Weren't you?'

'My motivation didn't seem to bother you much last
night.'

'I wanted you.' The raw confession made her body sway
like a sapling struck by an unexpected gust of wind. Her
nerves were vibrating like over-stretched violin strings. 'I
wasn't in a position to make conditions last night.'

'And you think you are now? This is my home, Ben, and
I decide who stays and who leaves. I'm not trying to pretend
last night didn't happen...' She wished he'd fasten his shirt;
it was making a difficult situation even more trying to be
faced with the expanse of golden-tanned skin.

'*Really?*'

'We should learn from our mistakes.'

'What a healthy, well-balanced attitude.'

'And I can do without your snide remarks,' she hissed,
hot-faced.

'Sorry,' he said unconvincingly. 'Tell me, what have you
learnt from our...*mistake*? Or are you just clearing the decks
for lover boy—off with the new, on with the old? Are you
really so sure he's still the right fit for you, Rachel? You
might discover you've done some growing.'

'I'm not trying to deny I find you physically attractive.'

'Pity; I could do with a good laugh.'

She refused to be sidetracked by his biting sarcasm.
'There's never been any question of anything more.' He'd
said as much by omission himself. 'The future doesn't really
come into the equation when we both know you're only here
for a matter of weeks. You were right...'

'There's a first time for everything.'

She gave a dignified sniff. 'When you said I'm not mistress material.'

'You think he'll leave his wife for you, because of Charlie? Grow up, Rachel; if having children meant more to him than her he'd have deserted her years ago. His sort always go back to the wife.'

'For God's sake,' she snapped, 'I'm not talking about being Christophe's mistress, I'm talking about being yours!'

He froze, and she had the fleeting impression he was biting back his instinctive response. When he spoke it was very slowly and precisely.

'I don't recall asking you.' Eyes narrowed, he rocked on the balls of his feet and stood waiting for the inevitable explosion.

She gave a gasp of anger. Of all the smug, arrogant, self-satisfied rats! 'There's no point in trying to be civilised with you, is there? Get out!' she yelled. 'Now!' *Mistress* was too formal a commitment for him! He thinks he can have me whenever he wants, and I haven't done much to discourage his theory so far, she thought bitterly.

Her anger seemed to have lifted his spirits; he grinned at her with every sign of pleasure. 'Are you going to throw that?' he enquired with interest, nodding at the hairbrush she was waving to emphasise her point.

'If I'm going to throw anything it will have a sharper edge than this.'

Still grinning, he shrugged on his jacket without bothering to fasten his shirt. The picture it presented was somehow decadent and erotic. Let's face it, girl, you'd find Ben Arden in a bin sack a turn-on; it's pathetic, simply pathetic, she told herself.

'For a woman who doesn't want to disturb the child you've turned the tiniest bit shrill.'

'You've not heard anything yet,' she promised grimly.

'Relax; I wouldn't dream of staying where I'm not welcome.'

'You finally got the message.'

'Put it down to the conflicting signals,' he said drily. Hand on the door handle, he turned back. 'Believe me, darling, it's your loss—I'm a morning man.'

The hairbrush hit the closed door.

CHAPTER SEVEN

'STOP there.' She must have this wrong. Fortunately he'd offered her a seat before he'd enlightened her as to the reason for this meeting or she might just have been stretched out on the ankle-deep Aubusson carpet by now.

There was no way Sir Stuart Arden could be saying what she thought he was. She'd probably feel extremely silly later for saying this.

'You want me to sleep with your son?'

She tried to make a joke of it but failed miserably; the persistent tremor reflected her bewilderment. He wasn't laughing and he wasn't looking furious at her presumption either.

'I didn't say that.'

'You implied it!' She was apparently to offer her body as inducement to Ben. Outrageousness seemed to be a congenital condition in the Arden family.

'You're a very blunt young woman, Miss French. I like that.' He beamed with generous approval at her.

'I thought I was unsuitable material for…' she began drily.

'I admit I might have been a bit hasty. I didn't like the idea of my son being saddled with a ready-made family.'

'I assure you that I'm not on the look-out for a rich husband—rich, or any other sort!'

'Since then I've been watching you.' Now there was a very unsettling thought, she reflected wryly. 'And I'm impressed by what I've seen.'

She judged it was time to put an end to this farcical situation. 'You've got this all wrong, you know. Ben isn't leaving because of me,' she said earnestly. As mistakes went this one was up there with the big boys. The ever-present bleakness settled around her heart like a steel band.

She could see she hadn't convinced him. It was made more difficult when he was pretty well sold on the popular theory of his own infallibility. When she'd been instructed to go to the big man's office several scenarios had crossed her mind—instant dismissal was one, a leave-my-son-alone lecture was another. Use your feminine wiles to make my son stay home hadn't been in the running!

'You're not the usual type he goes for at all.' Benedict's father obviously considered this a clinching argument but the significance remained unclear to Rachel. 'It's obvious he thinks he's in love.'

'Your son isn't in love with me.' She was able to say this without a blush; unfortunately she didn't have the same control over her heart as she did her complexion, and it hurt—it hurt a lot to actually acknowledge this.

With a slow nod of his head he conceded she might be right. It obviously didn't occur to him that it was tactless to concur. Rachel's exasperation was increasing by the second.

'He might *think* he is, though. He's not used to rejection.'

His surveillance network wasn't infallible, then. *Rejection!* Hysteria wouldn't be far away if she dwelt on that one too long!

'Benedict made this decision before he even came back to England.'

'Hah!' he said triumphantly. 'He's confided in you; I thought as much. Benedict doesn't do that—it just goes to prove it.'

'Prove what?'

'He's serious about you.'

'I really don't have any influence with your son.'

'You've got more than me.' For the first time she glimpsed

the depth of his frustration and anxiety. 'I'm asking you to use it to stop him making a terrible mistake. He'll thank us for it eventually.'

'I don't think Ben would thank anyone for conspiring behind his back.' If he ever found out about this little tête-à-tête she didn't want to be around.

'Conspiracy is a harsh word.'

'But accurate,' she insisted firmly.

Stuart Arden wasn't used to asking anyone for anything and it showed. She felt something she'd never imagined she'd feel for this man—she felt sympathy. It must have cost him a lot in pride to come to her and ask for her help. He must really be desperate to keep Ben in the country. However, she kept a tight hold on the sympathy; it wouldn't do to forget that behind the concerned father was a ruthless man who would do anything and use anyone to get his own way.

'I don't think Ben has taken this decision lightly.'

'Have you got any idea how gifted he is?' he asked, banging his fist down on the desk. 'He has a brilliant future to look forward to. He's throwing it all away! And for what? Some dry dustbowl!' he said scornfully. 'You must be able to see how ludicrous the idea is. This is a whim, nothing more. Do *you* want him to go?' She averted her face too slowly. 'I thought not.' He gave a triumphant grunt of satisfaction.

'What I want doesn't enter into it.'

'Are you lovers?'

Rachel got to her feet with as much dignity as she could muster. 'As my employer you have a number of rights, but asking that isn't one of them.'

'Don't be offended, my dear.' The transition from interrogator to kindly uncle was made with bewildering speed. 'If you want the man why don't you fight for him? You have weapons in your arsenal that I lack.'

Rachel's nostrils flared in annoyance. She didn't trust the crocodile smile one little bit. 'I think I should go,' she said firmly.

'A child—a baby—would make Benedict see where his responsibilities lie.'

Halfway to the door Rachel froze. She looked at the man behind the big desk with white-faced astonishment. 'Are you actually suggesting I get *pregnant* in order to keep Ben in the country?'

'It must have occurred to you.'

'You think so?' He *was* serious.

'There are in-built disadvantages to being a woman—no old-boy network, prejudices in the workplace—but there are also advantages, and I've always admired women who use their femininity to get what they want. A hint of cleavage can be just as affective as an old school tie.'

'Even if I did agree with you—which I don't—I hardly think what you're suggesting is comparable,' she croaked hoarsely.

'I'm only suggesting you utilise all the weapons at your disposal. If you don't like the idea of actually getting pregnant I understand. The mere possibility would be enough to bring him to his senses and lots of women lose babies...' His voice trailed off suggestively.

'You want me to pretend I'm pregnant?'

'Naturally I'd leave the details up to you.'

Her mouth worked and no sound came out. 'You expected me to go along with this idea?' All emotion was leached from her voice.

'Well, we both have something to gain.'

She took a deep, wrathful breath, her bosom swelling impressively as she did so. 'I'll *encourage* Ben to leave the country if it means he'll be clear of your devious machinations!' she announced, chin up, eyes blazing. 'What you've suggested is monstrous and immoral. I would never, *ever* use a child, or even,' she drawled sarcastically, 'the idea of a child, to trap a man. I think you've got a very warped idea of what love is, Sir Stuart. The sort of love I believe in doesn't manipulate and control a person.'

'Then you do love my son.' Sir Stuart looked thoughtful.

'I doubt very much if you know the meaning of the word.'

He laughed suddenly. 'You know, my wife said that to me the first time I proposed. She had that same look of disdain on her face when she said it, too,' he recalled with a nostalgic sigh.

'How did you get her to say yes? Threaten to bankrupt her father, or did you just kidnap her sick granny?'

To her amazement he appeared to find her sarcasm amusing. 'Perhaps she'll tell you one of these days, my dear. I hope there are no hard feelings; it was worth a shot. I'd do anything to keep Benedict from ruining his career,' he said simply.

'Maybe you justify your actions under the mantle of parental concern, but I don't swallow it. I think you're more concerned with how *you* feel, Sir Stuart.' She turned on her heel and left a very startled peer of the realm staring after her.

'Did Charlie really take the news well?'

'Better than I expected,' Rachel assured him. This evening was going better than she'd expected too. Christophe really was a pleasant companion. The natural awkwardness had faded quickly. He was an amusing, interesting companion, and a naturally kind man. 'She's fascinated by the idea of relations she's never met. I left her curled up with a book of French grammar—light reading, you know?' She laughed.

'A mixed blessing being so bright?'

She nodded at his perception. 'Sometimes,' she confessed.

'She milked me dry for details about your family. I hadn't realised until recently how much she wanted to know about her father. If I had...who knows?' She gave herself a sharp mental shake; it was never useful to reflect on paths you hadn't taken. 'I think she wants to interrogate you now.'

'You scare me.'

'I said she could stay up late to see you again—if you'd like.'

His smile deepened. 'I'd like. Annabel wanted to fly over, but I said it was probably better to play things slowly. I don't want to overwhelm her.'

'Charlie isn't easily overwhelmed,' Rachel said drily. 'But I think slowly is the best way to play this.'

'That looks marvellous.' Christophe breathed in the aroma appreciatively as the waiter placed his steaming dessert before him. 'Are you sure you're not tempted?' He rubbed his hands together in gleeful anticipation of the calorific delight.

Rachel grinned as he attacked the mammoth-sized portion with the enthusiasm of a schoolboy. 'I imagined we'd be dining somewhere very French,' she teased. The restaurant he'd brought her to specialised in traditional, unglamorous English cuisine.

'What could be more glamorous than a steamed suet pudding?' he asked indignantly, spoon poised halfway to his mouth. 'I have a weakness for English nursery food; do I have the expression right?'

She nodded. 'You have, only I imagine a cardiologist might have another name for it.'

'A little of what is bad for you occasionally can do no harm, Rachel.'

She was in a position to dispute that. A little of Ben had been *very* bad for her. Her concentration was shot to hell. It was getting hard to disguise the fact that she had no appetite. She had decided, rather harshly, that her face was looking quite gaunt tonight. As for sleep, she'd forgotten what it was to do anything other than toss and turn. It wasn't going to last, of course, she knew—she reminded herself of this fact a hundred times a day—only it didn't help.

She was just grateful for her premature return to Albert's office. Mr Arden apparently no longer had need of her services—or so the curt office memo had informed her. Pity he hadn't explained this to his father before she'd been subjected to that horrific interview, which got more bizarre and surreal every time she reconstructed it in her mind. She'd seen Ben just once in the distance; there had been no mistaking his broad back or the sound of Sabrina's high-pitched giggle.

'Will you have coffee?' Christophe asked for the third time.

'Sorry, I was miles away.' She unfolded her white knuckles from the wine glass and forced herself to smile. She wasn't about to tell him where she'd been or with whom. She listened as he patiently repeated himself.

'I do a passable coffee. Would you prefer to go back to my place? It will give you more time with Charlie.'

It was after midnight before she said goodnight to Christophe. She was only halfway up the stairs when the doorbell rang once more. He must have forgotten something she decided, skipping back down the stairs two at a time.

'What's...?' The smile died dramatically as she recognised the tall figure who loomed out of the darkness. 'Go away! Despite her determined attempts to close the door in Benedict's face the large size eleven got in the way. A well muscled thigh followed the foot and she found herself thrust back against an unattractive umbrella stand which stood in the hallway.

'Don't bother closing that door—you're leaving,' she said grimly.

'Not until you've done a bit of explaining.'

'You're the one who should be explaining. What do you think you're doing barging in here?'

'I waited until Fauré had left. I thought that was very considerate of me.' Benedict's affable expression was somewhat spoilt by the waves of anger emanating from his lean body.

'You've been skulking out there waiting!' she accused, going cold all over at the thought. 'Spying on me!' she squeaked in outrage.

'*I know.*'

Whatever he knew it didn't seem to be affording him much pleasure. In fact the pulse that visibly throbbed in his forehead looked about ready to pop. Explosive described fairly accurately his state of mind at the moment.

'I'm happy for you. At least I would be if I had the faintest idea what you were talking about.' She picked up the assorted umbrellas and placed them back in the Victorian stand.

Hands thrust deep in his jeans pockets, he looked down at her with open contempt. 'And I don't suppose you went to see my father either?' he said in a voice calculated to wither hardier blooms than Rachel.

She turned to face him, a red brolly still clutched in her bloodless grip.

'Did you think he wouldn't tell me?' Benedict noticed she'd gone bluish around the lips. The floor was hard, unyielding mosaic tile; he'd have to move fast if she fainted.

'Actually I didn't think he would,' she confessed eventually. Her head was spinning. Stuart Arden wasn't the sort of man who did anything unless he thought he could get something out of it. For the life of her she couldn't imagine what advantage he imagined this confession would give him.

'Why the hell did you go to him, not me?' he demanded in an anguished voice. He swept an impatient hand through his hair—hair that had been soaked by the light summer shower. Dampness made his shirt cling to the contours of his upper body, emphasising his powerful physique.

Rachel's confusion deepened. For some reason he seemed to think she'd instigated the interview. Was it possible that Sir Stuart had, for his own reasons, made her the instigator?

'I know you're angry, and I don't blame you, but you can't blame me.'

'Blame you?' he echoed blankly. The deep red coloration seeped slowly until it covered every scrap of his skin she could see. 'Is that what you think of me?' he asked hoarsely. 'You thought I'd be angry?'

'Well, you are angry, aren't you?' she pointed out, somewhat mystified by his reaction.

'Because you didn't tell me, not because you're—'

'But couldn't this have waited until morning, or better still Monday? I really do think you're overreacting, Ben.' Her thoughts raced as she tried to quell the rising sense of panic. If he came in, if he touched her... She had no will-power where he was concerned. One thing she knew she *couldn't* do was say goodbye again.

'You think I'm...' Words appeared to fail him at this point. 'I'm sorry if my emotional outburst offends you but it's not every day I learn I'm about to be a father. Perhaps you can be blasé about it, having been there once, but this is the first time for me.'

It was Rachel's turn to be rendered speechless. She tried to interpret his words first one way then another way, but the meaning kept coming out the same.

'You think I'm...? Your father told you I'm...?'

'For once in his life my father did the decent thing. Something you obviously don't think I'm capable of.'

The irony struck her as being hilariously funny. She laughed, a wobbly giggle that swiftly crossed the border into hysteria. In her youth she'd had to overcome this embarrassing response to moments of high emotional drama. Laughter had frequently caused offence at numerous delicate moments and she could see she hadn't lost her knack—he looked ready to throttle her!

'You find this situation funny?' he enquired coldly.

She gasped for breath. 'I'm hysterical, you idiot!' she gasped. She clutched her aching stomach muscles as tears began to run down her cheeks.

'Do you prefer right cheek or left?' he asked, touching her chin and examining each profile in turn. 'Isn't that the traditional remedy?'

'You w-wouldn't dare!' She hiccuped as she gradually regained control. He didn't deny or confirm this accusation, just smiled in what she considered to be a sinister manner.

'Didn't you think I had a right to know? Didn't you think I was sufficiently involved to be informed?' he grated sarcastically. 'You've already deprived one child of her father. I can't believe you were going to do it again. Well, whatever plans you had, Rachel, you'd better include me.'

'This is ridiculous, Ben. Will you listen to me?'

'I've accepted you think I'm some lightweight party animal with no depth, but did you *really* imagine that I wouldn't care if a woman was carrying my child?'

The way his eyes ran over her body and came to rest on her flat belly with a fierce, possessive expression made her feel...*excited*? That's sick, Rachel—stop it! she told herself firmly. This wasn't the time to forget this pregnancy was a fantasy spun by a devious, warped mind.

'Or did you just not take my feelings into consideration?'

'Oh, so this is all about *you*, is it?' Hands on her hips, she let her scornful glance travel to the top of his dark head. 'Your fragile male pride.'

'Miss French, are you all right?' Clad in pyjamas, the occupant of the ground-floor flat opened his door. 'It's just I heard some noise...' The retired accountant had to take a step back to see Benedict's face. He pushed his wire-framed spectacles up his thin nose and devoutly hoped Miss French wouldn't want any help.

'I'm really sorry we disturbed you and Mrs Rose,' Rachel began, wiping away the last remnants of moisture from her face. That might be the last time she laughed in a long time, she thought bleakly.

'I told her not to have the second bottle of wine. She gets a little...shrill when she's over-indulged,' Benedict said in conspiratorial undertones. 'We'll take ourselves upstairs. Do you need a hand, my love?' he enquired solicitously.

Rachel gritted her teeth and looked from the confused face of her neighbour to Benedict. If she didn't want to include half the neighbourhood in her troubles she didn't have much choice.

'I can manage, thank you,' she said from between clenched teeth as she shrugged off the hand on her elbow which was much more to do with restraint than solicitude.

The door upstairs was still ajar and she ducked under Benedict's arm as he held it open. *'Thank you,'* she grated sarcastically. 'God knows what he thinks now. He saw me go out with one man and come back with another!' she fumed.

'Worried about your reputation, Rachel? It's a bit late for that, isn't it?'

'I've done nothing to be ashamed of.'

'I'm pleased to hear it, because if you had...' He gave a thin-lipped smile and his eyes glittered as he let his glance dwell on her face. 'Shall we just say it saves me the bother of ruining his expensive dental work?'

'If I decide to sleep with the entire English soccer team it's nothing to do with you! Clean up your own act before you start interfering in mine.'

'Are you trying to tell me it's my debauched reputation

that's behind your decision to keep me in the dark?' he enquired cynically.

'What gives you the idea I'm even *slightly* interested in your reputation?' she enquired scornfully.

'I'm crushed,' he remarked, looking anything but. 'I've spent all my adult life polishing my depraved image. Is Charlie asleep?' he asked, looking around the room.

Rachel nodded reluctantly; after her late night Charlie had gone out like a light.

'She met Fauré?' His eyes touched the large elaborate bouquet on the dining table and his lip curled contemptuously. 'A little ostentatious,' he commented, with a quirk of one dark brow.

'They got on very well.' She wasn't about to tell him that Charlie's approval of Christophe had contained a significant rider: 'I don't like him as much as Ben.'

'You decided it was too complicated to cope with two fathers at the same time?'

'You're not my child's father, Ben.'

'Prospective father, if you're going to be pedantic.'

'I'm not pregnant, Ben.'

'Can't you do any better than that?' His scorn was corrosive enough to strip metal. 'Don't treat me like a fool, Rachel.'

'It's the truth.' What else could she say to convince him?

'Did you enjoy single parenthood so much you want to go through it again? Or are you hoping Fauré will accept this child as his too? If you have any ideas along those lines, Rachel, drop them now.'

She embraced the anger; it was easier to cope with than impotence. 'I shouldn't really blame you for sounding like a tinpot dictator. I suppose your father has always spoken to your mother like that. But if you use that tone with me once more, so help me...'

For the first time she saw a flicker of amusement. Momentarily it lifted the sombre expression on his strikingly handsome face.

'What's the joke?'

'After you've met my mother you'll understand.'

'I'm not going to meet your mother.'

His expression was the visual equivalent of a patronising pat on the head and she wanted to scream very badly. The only thing stopping her was the child sleeping in the next room.

'I suppose you were relying on the fact that I'll be leaving the country. You mistakenly thought that Dad would be on your side as he was so anxious to warn me off you. You miscalculated; one thing he feels passionate about is family!'

'Oh, I know all about your father's concern for his family. I'd say he'd go to any lengths to preserve it. Can you imagine your father as a cosy grandfather, Ben?' Anyone would think he *wanted* to believe his father's story.

'This is about us, not my father.' He pushed aside her dry observation impatiently.

'Would that were true.'

'He said you didn't intend telling him. He said you were very depressed and you just blurted it out.'

'"He said! He said!"' she mimicked, wishing the unscrupulous old man were here so she could tell him exactly what she thought of him. 'You're not listening to *me*, are you? How could I be pregnant?'

If he paused long enough to think he'd see that it wasn't possible. 'I told you the first time it was safe and then we took precautions.' She was annoyed that the reference made her flush like a schoolgirl, not a thirty-year-old mother. 'Besides, it was only three weeks ago.' The argument was pretty watertight, she thought, giving a relieved sigh. The relief proved premature, however, as she listened to Benedict proceeding to punch holes in her neat logic.

'The only fail-safe form of contraception is abstinence—we've not been very abstemious.'

Greedy, she decided, was a more accurate description; the thought brought an unwelcome reminder of the fact that some things hadn't changed. She still felt *greedy*. She lowered her eyes self-consciously before the scorching recognition surfaced in her eyes.

'And these days a testing kit can tell you if you're pregnant when you're hours late.'

'I wouldn't know.'

'I have friends who were desperate to get pregnant. Tom could have written a consumer column on kits that tell you when you should or shouldn't and others that tell you when you are or aren't. Or did you just know? Some women do.'

'Stop it!' she yelled, placing her hands firmly over her ears. 'I'm not pregnant! Your father was lying.'

'He can, and does, but why would he lie now? And why *this* lie? What would he have to gain?'

At last! Here was her opportunity to explain. 'He thinks if I get pregnant you won't leave the firm and you won't leave the country.' Even to her own ears the idea sounded preposterous.

'Is that the best you can do, Rachel? Why would he think that? I can't think of a better place in the world than the Creek to bring up a child.'

She would like to be watching when Benedict revealed this to his father. It wouldn't make up for what he'd done, but it would certainly help! Despite all his father's underhand tactics Benedict still had no intention of continuing with his legal career! At any other time the irony might have made her smile.

'Charlie will love it too,' Benedict continued persuasively. 'After we're married…'

'Married?' she echoed hollowly.

'I've no desire to be a part-time father, Rachel.' He looked at her as if he were stating the obvious and sank his fingers into the dark hair above a forehead pleated in a deep frown.

The gesture was implicitly weary; she could almost see him physically push aside the fatigue as his hand fell away. She had to do the same with the warm, mushy feelings that made her a push-over where he was concerned. He's tough, girl; he doesn't need you to mop his tired brow! she told herself.

'What happened to the "include me in your plans, Rachel"?' she enquired pointedly. 'Suddenly it seems as if *I* don't have any say in the matter.'

'Not a pleasant feeling, is it?' His resentment seemed momentarily overridden by concern as he examined her pale face. 'For God's sake, woman, sit down before you fall down.'

'Will you stop that? I don't want to sit down!' she snapped as he all but manhandled her into an oak carver chair she'd inherited from her aunt. Her hands curved around the smooth, worn wood of the arms; the solid familiarity was strangely comforting.

'You have to look after yourself,' he said gruffly, backing off.

This, she realised, was Benedict's version of the kid-glove treatment. She ignored the wistful sigh somewhere in the back of her mind. If this were for real it might be *quite* nice to be cherished by Ben Arden. The idea of carrying his child for real was dangerously seductive. Ever since his father had planted the germ of the idea she hadn't been able to stop imagining.

'I'm not ill!'

'Pregnancy isn't an illness,' he agreed gravely. 'Did you have an easy time with Charlie—any problems? I saw the scar.'

She started. Recalling the circumstances in which he'd noticed the almost invisible scar made her stomach muscles clench. Trying to cover her tingling breasts would only draw attention to the effect his casual words had had.

Though she didn't know why she was bothering; Ben had obviously already lost interest in her in *that* way. Naturally she'd been relieved when he hadn't continued to pursue her and Sabrina, by all accounts, was helping him fill his social calendar. Now she was nothing more than an incubator!

'I had a Caesarean.' Serve him right if she did treat him to the nitty-gritty.

'Does that mean that—?' he began uncooperatively, displaying much less embarrassment than she was feeling with the topic.

'I'm not pregnant, Ben,' she breathed, with an exasperated sigh. Much more of this and she was going to start believing it too!

'If you had a tough time I can understand why you want to deny it, but this is happening, Rachel.'

'I don't want your understanding! You're going to feel really stupid when you realise I'm telling the truth,' she said, not without relish.

'My God!' he said suddenly, his eyes narrowing in suspicion. 'You're not thinking of abortion, are you? Because I have to tell you... No, you couldn't do that.' Just as she was getting ready to throw something large and painful at him his expression cleared. 'You wouldn't.' His sudden supreme confidence brought a lump of emotion to her throat.

'I don't know what to say,' she sniffed, and found a man-sized handkerchief pushed into her hand. Nothing short of divine intervention, it seemed, would convince him she wasn't pregnant.

'I know.'

'You don't, Ben.'

'I do. I was shocked, especially when I heard it from the source I did. It's not something I'd planned to happen right now.'

Or ever, she thought, quite touched by this display of consideration for her feelings.

'But the idea of the life I planted growing in you...it's... The whole idea is *incredible*,' he grated thickly.

Something moved deep inside her as she listened to the depth of emotion throbbing in his voice. He dropped to his knees and gripped her thighs. It was impossible to look away from his searching eyes.

'If by incredible you mean implausible I couldn't agree more,' she croaked.

'By incredible I mean astounding, miraculous, wonderful, extraordinary—' His big hands tightened around her slim thighs.

'There's nothing extraordinary about pregnancy; it's commonplace.'

'Not for me, Rachel. I want to share this. Don't try and push me away.'

The stumbling analysis of her feelings revealed a shocking truth—she wanted it to be true. Part of her wished that his child were growing in her belly. Part of her wanted to have a legitimate reason to follow him to Australia, start a new life together. Was this what his father had reckoned on—her weakness?

Right now he didn't love her, but he didn't hate her either, and he would if she was crazy enough to follow her baser instincts.

'Leaving aside the fact I'm not pregnant for the moment,

what makes you think that I'd want to follow you to the other side of the world? I know there's a body of opinion that still thinks, even in this enlightened age, that a woman should follow her man...' She filled the pause with light laughter and saw the muscles around his sensual mouth tighten. 'But even they would agree that these extravagant acts of sacrifice have to be inspired by love. We've shared a lot of unbridled lust,' she said candidly, 'but *love*? I think I'd have remembered if you'd dropped that into the conversation.'

'And if I had?' It was hard to tell from his expression if he'd found her frankness insulting.

In my dreams you did... 'You didn't, I didn't and I'm not marrying anyone I don't love.'

'Then perhaps I'll just have to make you love me.' She had the impression she'd succeeded in getting under his guard this time. Seeing the implacable light in his eyes, she wasn't so sure this had been an altogether sensible thing to do.

'Don't be stupid.'

'You sound nervous, Rachel.'

'I'm not nervous, I'm tired. You can't *make* someone fall in love. They either do or they don't.' *I should know.*

'Then you've nothing to worry about, have you?'

'I'm not worried. As for this talk of marriage, you'll realise shortly that it was just a knee-jerk reaction.'

'Would it surprise you to learn I've been thinking of getting married quite a lot recently?'

'Yes,' she said flatly, 'it would. If you're going to wheel out some pathetic story that you're really desperately in love with me—don't!'

An expression she didn't understand flickered across his face. 'Did I say it was you I was considering marrying?' Head tilted slightly back, eyes half closed, there was nothing lazy about the way he watched her.

She stuck out her chin and determined to tough out the wave of hot mortification. 'You have a novel way of making a girl fall in love with you.'

'I'm trying to lull you into a false sense of security.'

'It's a mistake to reveal your tactics. As for security, just think how secure I'll feel when you start taking other women out.'

His lips twitched as he acknowledged her saccharine-sweet words. 'Sabrina is a lovely girl, but can you see her on an isolated property in the outback? You've no need to feel jealous of Sabrina.'

'You're on the look-out for a female with a strong back and good child-bearing hips? I'm flattered.'

'That's an interesting suggestion. Especially the bit about the hips.' His hands slid upwards until his thumbs came into contact with the sharp, jutting crests that delineated her slim pelvis. Through the contact he felt the shiver that affected her entire body. He smiled. 'And you've already got a proven track record in the fertility stakes.' He shook his head slowly and grinned at her outraged little gasp.

'I think I might have given you a false impression of the Creek, Rachel. The conditions are not exactly primitive, you know. And whilst we are isolated a plane really does cut down the distances. Despite what my father likes to imply, it's not exactly a tin shack and life is a long way from being a cultural desert.'

'You can fly?' She was fascinated despite herself. It was something she'd always wanted to learn.

'Nina, my grandmother, gave me flying lessons for my eighteenth birthday. I got the bug, which was no doubt what she intended. In her own way Nina was as crafty as my father; she made no secret of the fact that she wanted me to take over from her.'

'And now you are.'

'She's probably up there somewhere laughing.'

'Pardon me for not joining in with the merriment but being treated like a pregnant piece of livestock has had a detrimental effect on my sense of humour.'

'You didn't think I was serious for one minute,' he chided. 'At least you're not denying it now—the fact that you're pregnant. That's something.'

'I am not!'

'I'd say, Are too, but I'm trying to create a mature and responsible impression.'

'Are you implying I'm being immature?'

He anchored her flailing arms securely in his hands before replying. 'I'm saying that you being pregnant changes things whether you like it or not,' he said soberly.

And, despite his assurances to the contrary, he *didn't* like. Nothing he'd said or done had convinced her otherwise.

'You've done a good—no, a *great* job of bringing up Charlie, but you know better than most that a child needs two parents.'

'Two *loving* parents.'

'We can love pretty sensationally.'

'I'm not talking about *sex*,' she said witheringly. 'Even *sensational* sex isn't a basis for marriage!' She examined the foot she'd just unintentionally directed a bullet at and winced.

'Thank you, Rachel; I thought it was too.' He looked as smug as your average sleek predator when it sank its claws into dinner. 'Charlie likes me too.'

'That's really low—using a child's feelings.'

'I'm telling it the way it is, Rachel,' he said with no trace of remorse. 'Charlie would be better off with me providing the male influence in her life. You've got to admit Fauré isn't much of an improvement on a test-tube!'

'Isn't that the tiniest bit inconsistent? You're the one getting all defensive about a biological father's rights.'

'He's married. He forfeited any rights he might have had,' he said, nostrils flared in distaste. 'That's a fact I intend to convey to your friend very soon.'

'No! You can't do that!' she gasped. She could imagine poor Christophe's reaction if he thought she was spreading the story that he was Charlie's father. What if the story got back to Annabel?

'I'll make a deal. I'll keep away from Fauré for now if you agree to stop pretending. I can't talk to you about practical arrangements if you keep denying you're pregnant.'

She bit back the denial. Perhaps it would be sensible to go along with him, just for tonight, if it meant keeping him from confronting Christophe! Tomorrow she was going to confront Stuart Arden and make him confess that he'd been lying through his teeth.

'Practical arrangements?'

'Obstetrician's appointments; I'd like to come with you.'

'I haven't got an obstetrician.'

'Have you been to see a doctor at all?' He frowned in disapproval when she shook her head. 'Well, firstly I think we should—'

'I'm sure you're right, Ben, but I'm really very tired right now.' It wasn't hard to convey lassitude when mentally she was close to complete exhaustion. She saw the concern on his face and felt a spasm of guilt when he touched a solicitous hand to the side of her face.

'Tomorrow, then?'

She nodded mutely; the impulse to turn her cheek lovingly into his open palm was overwhelmingly strong. Her feelings were ambiguous when he did remove his hand.

After he'd let himself out of the flat she could feel the impression where his fingers had touched her face. Even the dampness from the tears didn't diminish the sensation.

CHAPTER EIGHT

'SIR STUART isn't at home.'

'I'll wait.' Boldly Rachel stepped into the vast hallway. Her heels echoed on the marble floor. She glanced casually around; this wasn't the moment to be intimidated by insignificant things like chandeliers the size of her living room and several paintings by an artist she'd never seen outside a museum.

'I'm afraid, madam, that won't be possible.'

Rachel squared her chin; it was going to take more than a sneer from a professional flunky to put her off. 'If you tell him I'm here he'll see me.'

'Is there a problem, David?'

Rachel automatically looked in the direction of the light musical voice. Tall and slim with dark red hair tied back in a ponytail at the nape of her neck, the figure on the curved staircase ran gracefully down the remaining steps. She was dressed for riding and the scarf at her neck was the same vivid green as her eyes.

'This person wishes to see Sir Stuart.'

'This person', Rachel thought, her lip curling. How delightfully 'Jeeves'.

'I have told her he isn't at home. I don't know how she got past Security.'

Rachel held up the official-looking papers in her hand bearing the authentic letterhead of the chambers. 'I said I was a messenger from the office.' She didn't want anyone to get into trouble on her account.

'And aren't you?' the redhead asked with interest.

'I work there.'

'For my husband?'

Husband! Rachel blinked. 'You can't be!' she repudiated
hotly, feeling as if a fist had been jabbed into her solar
plexus.

Aware that the lady of the house was regarding her with
concern tinged by alarm—and who could blame her?—she
tried to re-establish herself as a reasonably safe person to
open the door to. When she paused to think, not react, her
mistake was obvious. No, if Ben had had a wife, especially
one as photogenic as this, it would hardly have escaped public notice.

'You look too young to be Ben's mother,' she added impetuously when she had established the woman's identity by
means of elimination. 'That is, I thought you'd be—' Stop
while you've only one foot in your mouth, Rachel, she told
herself. Nothing so far was going according to her mental
plan. She just hoped her words hadn't been interpreted as an
attempt to ingratiate herself. The thought made her cringe.

It was unsettling to have her mental image of a well-bred
doormat replaced by the vibrant, confident woman before her.

'I am Emily Arden. You work for Ben, do you? Is it him
you're looking for?'

'No! I don't want to see him!' Horror-struck at the possibility that he might appear, she couldn't prevent herself
from glancing nervously over her shoulder.

'Then you'll be pleased to hear he's not at home.' If she
felt surprise at her visitor's obvious aversion to the notion of
seeing her son her polite expression didn't reveal it.

Rachel's tension eased down a notch. 'I really do need to
see Sir Stuart. It's personal.'

'About a personal matter? Should I be worried?'

Rachel looked at her blankly for a moment before blushing
vividly. 'Not that sort of personal.'

'I'm only teasing, my dear. My husband has many faults, but chasing young women is not one of them. One of them, however, is a habit of becoming invisible when it suits him,' she added drily.

'Are you saying he's not at home?' Rachel tried to keep her voice steady and failed. He *had* to be here. He had to explain to Benedict. She'd worked herself up to this confrontation and now the anticlimax was tremendous. She suddenly felt a feeble shadow of the strong positive, young woman who'd sailed in here on a cloud of determination.

'Why don't you come through and have a drink, my dear? You look as though you need it. Look after these, David.' She took the file of papers from Rachel's limp grasp and handed them to the butler. 'Could you organise some coffee in the drawing room? Come along.' Rachel found herself meekly falling in step with the lady of the house.

'It's a lovely room,' Rachel said miserably on entering the drawing room.

'Yes, isn't it?' She noticed Rachel's eyes were fixed on an aerial photograph set in an elaborate frame. 'I was born there,' she said with an affectionate smile.

'Connor's Creek?' When Benedict had said it wasn't a tin shack he hadn't been joking. She could have lived there, she thought, gazing at the well laid out paddocks around the sprawling house. If she'd been willing to lie and cheat, that was.

'That's right. I'm afraid it isn't so green just now.' Emily Arden recovered her composure smoothly. The unhappy young woman's instant recognition had surprised her. 'Sit there; that's right. Now, tell me why you need to see my husband.'

'I need him to tell Ben the truth; he won't believe me.' If she'd been truly prepared she'd have had a cover story ready; as it was, the truth would have to do.

'What won't he believe?'

'That I'm not pregnant.'

The green eyes blinked twice and the slim, beautifully manicured hand gripped the chintz-covered chair-arm a little more firmly, but that was the only visible response to this statement.

'Perhaps I'm a little slow, but why does he think you are?'

'Because his father told him I am,' she choked.

'Isn't that just typical of Stuart? He creates chaos and leaves me to sort it out!' Emily Arden folded her arms across her bosom and pursed her lips. 'He does insist on meddling.'

Rachel stared; she couldn't quite believe the older woman's ready acceptance of her story. She hadn't even asked why her husband would do such a bizarre thing.

'You believe me?' she said incredulously. 'I could be anyone. I walk in here saying I'm—'

'I know; it's a shock. As a mother of two sons I was always prepared for a girl to walk in and announce she was pregnant, but to say she's not! I didn't have the speech prepared for this eventuality.'

'It's not a joke.'

The attractive face melted into a smile that was so kind, Rachel had to bite her lip to hold back the tears. 'I can see that, my dear; forgive me.'

'It's awful,' Rachel sniffed. 'He wants to marry me,' she explained in an outraged tone.

The dark eyebrows lifted towards the smooth hairline, but her serene expression stayed intact. *'Really?'*

'Only because of the baby.'

'But there is no baby.'

'Try telling him that. He won't take no for an answer.'

An expression of irritation flashed across Emily Arden's face as the sound of voices through the open French doors grew louder. 'Dry your eyes, my dear,' she advised softly. 'I think we're about to be invaded. I think you'd better tell me your name before I introduce you to the rest of the family.'

'Rachel—Rachel French.'

'Nat, darling, don't bring those animals in here; they smell disgusting.'

'I like wet-dog smell.' The tall, dark-haired teenager looked curiously at Rachel. 'Hi!'

'This is Rachel French; she works with your brother. Rachel, this is Natalie, and this is Tom, my eldest.' The slim, auburn-haired man carrying a sleeping toddler smiled warmly at her. 'And his wife, Ruth.' Ruth had hair the same pale colour as the sleeping child; she also had a lovely smile. 'Oh, and this is Sabrina—a friend of the family.'

Rachel wasn't sure whether wishful thinking supplied the certain reserve in the older woman's voice when she made her final introduction.

'I've seen you somewhere. I know, you're the secretary person.' This discovery was expressed in a bored, well-bred drawl. 'Is Ben here too?' Sabrina asked, her voice suddenly much more animated than it had been.

'I'm afraid not,' their hostess said smoothly. 'A family get-together without two male members of the family and with the addition of two unexpected guests. Par for the course,' she observed philosophically.

'I'm not staying,' Rachel said, getting to her feet. Her skin wasn't really thick enough for this intrusion stuff. If Sir Stuart wasn't here there wasn't much point in her staying, and there was always the worrying possibility that Ben would appear. 'In fact I think I should go now. I'm very sorry to intrude.'

'Here's coffee now. You must join us. I insist.' Beneath the smile Rachel could see the definite glint of steely determination. At least Sir Stuart didn't get entirely his own way at home. This thought offered her small comfort as she desperately tried to think of a reason for her immediate departure.

'But my friend is picking me up.' She glanced down at her wristwatch to illustrate the imminence of this event.

'Well, we'll get them to send him up to the house when he arrives. It is a he?'

'Yes. His name's Fauré.' She decided to be gracious in defeat.

'French!' The dark-haired daughter of the house pushed a dog off the sofa and installed herself cross-legged in its place. 'I think continental men are simply delicious. So much more sexy than boring Brits.' She flashed her brother a meaningful glance. 'Especially Frenchmen. All my lovers shall be French or maybe Italian.'

'Thanks a lot,' her brother said drily. 'I'll just take Libby up to bed; she's due her nap.' He patted the sleeping child on his shoulder gently on the back. He murmured a soft aside to his wife and she nodded.

'Get them to ring down to the gate about Rachel's friend, Tom.'

'Will do.' He nodded, before turning his attention briefly back to his sister. 'If I can't excel as a Latin lover—' he struck a mock-heroic pose and then slumped his shoulders pathetically '—I'll just have to earn my keep being useful round the house. Incidentally, Nat, maybe you should wait until you've got the ironwear off the teeth before you start working your way through the continental studs. A moment of passion and their crowns could be dust.'

'Shut up, you; I don't know how Ruth puts up with you!' his sister yelled after him. 'I shall have beautiful teeth,' she observed, tapping the metal framework around her front teeth.

'You will, my dear,' her mother confirmed. 'Ah,' she said,

inclining her head to one side in an attentive attitude. 'I recognise that slam. I do believe Benedict is back.'

'Oh, excellent.' Sabrina got to her feet slowly and regarded
her reflection in an ornate mirror on the wall opposite with
a smug smile.

Rachel got to her feet, too, like a puppet whose strings had
just been jerked particularly viciously, but she wasn't smiling. She was still wondering if she could make it safely
through the French windows before he entered the room
when the door was pushed open.

'Darling.'

'Sabrina, what are you doing here?' Benedict's response
would have dampened more sensitive spirits than Sabrina,
who smiled seductively and glided across the room. 'Good
God, *Rachel*!' He literally froze.

Someone released the tension on those invisible strings and
her knees started to quiver. 'I'm just going, Mr Arden.' Her
voice showed a tendency to quiver too. She heard it and
Benedict did too; she watched his lips curve into a cruel
smile. He looked to be in one hell of a temper.

'*Mr Arden?*' he echoed mockingly. '*Miss French*, no,
you're not leaving!'

'Really, Ben, darling, it is the weekend; I'm sure the girl
has better things to do than—do whatever secretaries do.'

Sabrina, Rachel thought despairingly, was probably the
only person in the room that hadn't read, and personally
translated, the undercurrents. Lurid reading those versions
probably made, too.

'I'm not his secretary!'

'She's not my secretary!'

The two hot denials emerged simultaneously and seething
grey eyes clashed with smouldering brown ones.

'What is she, then? And why is she here?' asked the

blonde, with a disgruntled expression. She didn't like conversations that didn't include herself.

The crinkly lines Rachel loved around Benedict's eyes deepened as he regarded her with narrow-eyed interest. 'Good question. What are you, and why are you here, Rachel?'

He was gloating, enjoying her discomfiture. Later, when she was rehashing the day's events, she might be able to come up with the perfect cutting rejoinder that would wipe that smug grin off his face, but right now she had to rely on the transparent subterfuge which had got her in here.

'I brought some papers for your father to sign.'

'What papers? Where are they?' He looked around the room, apparently confident he wouldn't discover any.

'I expect they're on your father's desk, Benedict. You look terrible.' Rachel thought he looked sinfully gorgeous but she could see what his mother meant. His eyes were definitely bloodshot and he hadn't shaved; in fact he looked more like Charlie's guardian angel than the sleek legal eagle. 'What have you been doing with yourself?'

Rachel shot a grateful glance in Emily Arden's direction. She needed all the support she could get.

'I've spent the best part of two hours camped out on Rachel's doorstep.'

'You can hardly hold me responsible,' Rachel said indignantly in response to his smouldering glare. 'If you choose to waste your time that's your affair.'

'Talking of affairs...' he drawled.

He wouldn't! The dark eyes shone mockingly back at her. *He would!* Her stomach churned in misery and embarrassment. 'What am I supposed to do—wait in on the off chance you might want me?'

'I don't think there's any *might* about it.' His wry tone left no room for misinterpretation. She knew what he was thinking as his eyes made the journey from her toes to the top of her head with dramatic pauses to enjoy certain aspects of her figure, and so did everyone else in the room! She'd never felt so humiliated in her life—or as angry!

The slow, contemplative smile on his face broadened as the hot colour flared in two angry bands of red across her cheekbones.

'If you don't care about my feelings you might at least have the common courtesy not to embarrass your family,' she choked furiously. The bland look she received in return didn't display any signs of remorse.

'I'm not embarrassed,' Natalie observed chirpily.

An expression of shocked comprehension crossed Sabrina's face. 'But she's...' Her perfect nose wrinkled in confusion as she compared her own willowy reflection in the mirror with Rachel's slightly shorter, more curvy figure.

'*She's* going,' Rachel snapped. She didn't need the blonde to remind her of the disparity in their claims to beauty. And unlike Sabrina there was no way she could ever hope to match Benedict's sophistication. How he must be cursing the moment of madness that had tied him to her. She could imagine how relieved he'd be when he knew that there was no need to do the 'right thing'. His father certainly knew which buttons to press, she thought bitterly; Benedict wasn't the most obvious candidate for old-fashioned values.

'Not till I say so, you're not,' he replied in a cold, clear voice from which old-fashioned chivalry was noticeably absent.

Rachel heard a collective startled gasp and a nervous giggle, but she didn't notice from where it had originated. Her head was filled with the dull roar of the blood pounding in her ears.

'I'll go when and where I like, and if you try to stop me you can...'

'I can what?' he goaded.

She looked around and saw that all the audience was waiting for her answer with bated breath. Well, he might not mind providing a floor show for his nearest and dearest but she did!

'You know something, Ben? Meeting you is right up there with mumps and acne. You're the most insensitive, self-centred, manipulative...' She made a sound of disgust low in her throat. 'I wouldn't marry you if my life depended on it.'

'What makes you think it doesn't?' If anything the aggressive tilt of his square jaw had grown even more pronounced.

'You were right, Ruth. I owe you a tenner. He proposed! Well, I'll be—'

'Tom!' Benedict snarled, evincing no sign of brotherly love as he swung around to face the man who'd entered the room behind him. 'As a matter of fact I have. I've proposed and been refused. Thinking of offering me advice, are you?'

The eldest of the Arden brood bit back a grin and arranged his mobile features into a suitably sombre mask. 'Actually I just came to tell Miss French—Rachel—that her lift is here.' His green eyes sparkled with lively interest.

'Show him in, Tom,' Emily Arden instructed. 'Them in,' she corrected herself drily as the door swung open and Charlie walked in, followed at a more sedate pace by her uncle.

Charlie looked calmly around the room, completely unfazed by the unknown faces. 'This place looks like something off a magazine cover,' she remarked admiringly. She grinned at her mother. 'Hi, Mum!'

'She must be *old*.' Sabrina's chagrin was almost comical. She looked indignantly from Rachel to Charlie and back to Rachel again as if she expected to see her age before her eyes.

It was then that Charlie saw Benedict.

'Ben!' Her small face lit up and she ran like a heat-seeking missile straight at him.

That's what I want to do. Rachel felt the dull pain of acknowledgement. For a split second all she felt was deep envy for the ability to display such spontaneous pleasure.

Hiding her feelings meant she had to consider every word, every gesture. The expression on Benedict's face as he bent forward and lifted her high brought a heavy, emotional constriction to her aching throat. There could be no doubting the genuine nature of his feelings where Charlie was concerned.

His family watched with varying degrees of shock as Benedict swung the youngster up into the air before placing her back down on her feet and ruffling her halo of damp golden-blonde hair.

'I was wondering where you were.' He saw for the first time who had followed Charlie into the room. It was as if someone had flicked a switch. He was projecting such intense hostility, you could almost see the waves of loathing emanating from his eyes.

'I was with Uncle Christophe.' Charlie's vivid blue eyes turned happily to the figure who had so far been silent. 'We went swimming.'

'Ah, yes, *Uncle* Christophe.' His dark eyes met Rachel's. The contempt she read there made her jaw tighten and her chin go up in automatic defiance.

He obviously thought she'd created another story to spare herself Charlie's awkward questions, but she couldn't squash his nasty theory without revealing the fact that she'd let him believe a lie. Her glance moved worriedly to Christophe and she wondered how the older man would respond to Ben's hostility. She knew she only had Charlie's presence to thank for Benedict's restraint so far.

'Charlie is an excellent swimmer.' Christophe smiled warmly at his niece.

'When I go to France I shall swim in the sea—it's warm there—won't I, Mum?' Not daring to look in Benedict's direction, Rachel nodded weakly.

'And when is this trip arranged, Charlie?' Benedict asked, no discernible expression on his face.

There was no question of drawing blood from a stone; Charlie was only too happy to reveal her plans to Ben. Rachel listened with deepening resignation as her daughter told him their plans in tiresomely meticulous detail.

'Wouldn't it be great if Ben could come too, Mum?'

That really did focus her attention!

'Great!' she echoed hollowly. 'But he's a very busy man and he'll probably be in Australia by then.' She met the glittering mockery in Benedict's eyes with as much dignity as she could muster.

'My schedule is flexible.'

'My plans aren't.'

'We have an open house; any friend of yours is welcome, Rachel.'

She silently mouthed 'no' to Christophe and grimaced to indicate this wasn't a good idea. All her furtive pantomime achieved was to make Christophe look even more confused. She wished now that she'd given him an explanation for her trip here this morning.

With her luck the way Benedict's mind was working he'd probably think poor Christophe was inviting him to form part of some sort of *ménage à trois*! Before Rachel could divert Christophe's native hospitality Benedict spoke up.

'Open...?' he mused slowly. The derision seeped around the edges of his languid drawl and Rachel instinctively moved to stand protectively in front of Christophe. 'Myself,

I like boundaries. In homes, in jobs, most importantly in marriages. It cuts down on confusion.'

Christophe Fauré looked bemused and Rachel could understand why. She just hoped he'd stay that way. As he was completely innocent of marital infidelity, Benedict's heavy-handed irony wasn't likely to prick his conscience.

'Why doesn't Ben like Uncle Christophe?' There was an embarrassed silence as Charlie glanced enquiringly at her mother. She tugged imperatively at the loose white shirt Benedict wore tucked into his blue denims. 'He's nice, Ben.'

'I'm sure he is, Charlie.' He visibly reined in his aggression. He flexed his fingers as they unfurled from the balled fists which had rested suggestively at his sides. His breathing was almost normal as he smiled reassuringly down at the child.

'Well, I think Frenchmen are very nice.' Natalie got to her feet and crossed the room towards her brother. Her mother smiled on proudly as, displaying maturity beyond her years, her daughter successfully took the spotlight off her sibling.

'Thank you, *mademoiselle*.'

'I'm Natalie.' With a self-confident smile she extended her hand and eyed this mature example of the breed with open approval. She gave a laugh of delight as it was raised to his lips. 'Watch and learn, boys,' she advised her brothers.

'Are you Ben's sister?' Charlie asked curiously.

'For my sins.'

'You look alike.'

'So I've been told,' she replied, with a grimace. 'But, unfortunately, he's much prettier than me.'

'You're too kind,' her brother responded drily.

'Do you like horses, Charlie?' Natalie continued in her friendly manner. She squatted down until she was at eye level with the little girl. 'I was just on my way out to the stables...'

'I used to ride,' Charlie explained, her eyes sparkling in response. 'But we live in the town now.'

'Would you like to come and see them?'

'I'm afraid we've intruded long enough.' Rachel ignored the reproachful spaniel look her daughter threw in her direction. 'Christophe has an appointment in town this afternoon.' If he didn't pick up her desperate signals this time she'd just die.

'Yes, unfortunately I do need to leave.'

Rachel sighed with relief and sent him a grateful smile.

'That's no problem; I can give you and Charlie a lift back later, Rachel. I was going that way anyway.'

Fear was supposed to sharpen your wits, lend an extra edge to your mental faculties. I must be the exception to the rule, she thought, unable to tear her eyes away from Benedict's gaze. The insolence in those dark eyes was deliberate; he was daring her to get out of that one. She'd have loved to rise to the occasion but her brain was the consistency of mush.

'I...that is....'

'That's settled, then. Shall I show Mr Fauré to the door?'

'It's a bit late to play the perfect host, Benedict,' his mother said lightly. 'Mr Fauré, let me do the honours and possibly persuade you to come and visit again when things are less...' she eyed her son thoughtfully '...volatile?'

'Come on, Charlie,' Natalie said, chivvying the dogs with a piercing whistle. 'We'll go and see the horses.' She leant close to her brother. 'This will cost you big,' she said softly.

'I know.' Benedict's eyes didn't leave Rachel's face for an instant.

'And I expect a blow-by-blow—'

Benedict did look at her then with indulgent tolerance. 'Get a life, Nat,' he advised, not unkindly.

'Some chance of that; you want to try being sixteen,' she

tossed back, taking Charlie by the hand and leading her out into the garden.

'Weren't you going to show us those photos of the big bash for your brother's engagement, Sabrina?' Tom shot a slightly apologetic look towards his wife as he pulled her to her feet. 'Ruth was amazed when I told her who was there.'

This was enough to draw Sabrina's resentful eyes from the silent tableau of the two remaining figures in the room. 'Did I tell you that…?' She began ticking off all the minor members of royalty and media personalities who had been there on her carmine-tipped fingers. 'And she's much fatter than she looks on TV.' Rachel never did discover who this was: the doors in the Arden mansion were very solid.

'Alone at last.'

'I didn't say goodbye to Christophe. He'll think…'

Benedict's expression grew harsh, his jaw clenched in anger and his eyes were obsidian-hard. 'He's history,' he said with a dismissive shrug. 'And if he's got an ounce of intuition he knows it, and if he hasn't…' His sensual lips thinned to an unpleasant line.

She could hardly believe this was the same man with a solution to the most complex of legal problems who was displaying an amazing willingness to solve this problem with his fists. Violence was implicit in every line of his athletic, power-packed body.

'How dare you act like a…a barbarian? And if you touch me I'll scream…' she warned, backing away in panic as he moved towards her. If he touched her it would only be a matter of time—very little time—before she was begging—and this time she wouldn't be pleading for him not to touch her…

'As a family our mating rituals tend to be noisy; I don't think anyone will come running.'

'I'm not interested in your family.'

'Shame; they seem to like you. Of course it wouldn't make any difference if they didn't, but on the whole it makes matters simpler if they like my wife.'

'Ben.'

'Yes?' An odd expression flickered into his eyes as he looked down at her hands curled tightly in the fabric of his shirt. Her head was downbent, as though she couldn't bear to look at him. The tension in her slender body was palpable.

How did you convince someone of your sincerity? She closed her eyes tightly and willed him to hear the truth in her words. 'I'm *not* pregnant.'

'I know.'

Her eyes snapped open. 'What did you say?' Wide-eyed and confused, she finally lifted her eyes to his face.

'I know you're not pregnant.' He deftly untied the ribbon that confined her silky hair at the nape of her neck. 'That's better,' he reflected thickly as he spread it carefully over her shoulders. The delicate friction of his fingers on her scalp fragmented her residual concentration. He gently blew a stray strand that had settled on her cheek.

The warm scent, the teasing reminder of the taste of him made her ache; lips parted, she gasped for air. His fingers framed her face and firmly he pressed his lips to hers. It was all giving, no taking. The tenderness brought the sting of tears to her eyes.

'I tracked Dad down, and he admitted the truth—well, his version at any rate. I suspect I got a strictly censored version. He skated around the stuff that might reflect him in a less than favourable light.'

'That doesn't leave much.'

Was he feeling sorry for her? Was that why he was being so gentle? He realised how much she'd wanted it to be true? God, but she couldn't bear his pity.

This is what I wanted, she told herself. Mission accomplished. That was it, it was over; she could relax. She could get on with her life. Why wasn't she feeling better? Benedict was; he was looking positively smug. He was free. She knew she'd never be free from this love—not ever! It was a life sentence.

'My father has a gift with words,' Benedict admitted wryly.

'You must be relieved.'

'Must I?' The way he was looking at her made her sluggish heart shift into a higher gear. Other parts of her body followed suit and she rubbed the sudden rash of gooseflesh over her upper arms briskly. She dropped her eyes self-consciously from his and laughed lightly.

'It's quite funny when you think about it.'

'The humour escapes me right now.'

'Don't be too hard on him; I think he genuinely thinks he was doing what was best for you.'

'He always does. You seem very forgiving considering what a hard time I gave you because of his manipulative power games.'

She shrugged lightly and realised she was clinging again to his shirt-front. She let go and made an attempt to smooth down the crumpled areas. 'Sorry; it looks like you've been mauled,' she fretted.

He captured her hand mid-pat. 'I've got one or two others.'

'Of course you have.'

'And you can maul me whenever you feel the urge.'

The words turned on that X-rated Technicolor projector in her head and it became necessary to talk. It didn't much matter what she said or if it made sense; she just had to do something to distract herself.

'You can start your new life with a clean slate now. Just the way you planned. You're not...lumbered with excess baggage.' She tried to sound generous and optimistic even if the idea made her feel wretched inside.

'Would it have been so very terrible?' His warm fingers curled around her chin again. His dark, beloved face swam mistily through the fog of hot, unshed tears.

'I don't have the excuse of youth this time.'

'Do you need an excuse?'

'To do what? Be reckless and irresponsible?'

'No, to have my baby.' His hand slid down to rest on her flat stomach. Her eyes were riveted on the warm, intimate image. Her body was screaming out with need. The tears she'd held back successfully suddenly began to fall in earnest.

'You don't know how horrible I am,' she sobbed. 'I wished it was true.' She bent her head and burrowed into the hard, unyielding wall of his chest. The solidity and strength of it were somehow comforting. 'I was actually tempted to let you believe…' She bit down hard on her quivering lower lip and lifted her head, prepared for his scorn. 'Your father is a good judge of character.' There, it was out! Her dark secret was there for all to see.

'So did I.' Benedict was clearly still fixated on her earlier comment.

'You…? I don't understand,' she faltered. The solid ground she was standing on suddenly felt like shifting sand. What he was saying made no sense, unless…? No. She closed her mind firmly against this miraculous, impossible idea.

'I wished it was true too. That's why it took so long for me to see you were telling the truth. I wanted you to be carrying my baby. I thought I could use it as a lever to make you stay with me. Every time I tried to tell you how I felt you pushed me further away. I was so frightened of pushing too hard and losing you completely.' The memory of the pain still lingered like a shadow in his dark eyes.

He caught hold of her cold hand and raised it to his mouth. His eyes were half closed as his open lips moved over her palm. 'Marry me, Rachel,' he said, his voice throbbing with emotion. 'If you really hate the idea of Connor's Creek we could stay here in England. It doesn't really matter where we are so long as we're together,' he said urgently.

'I love you, darling, and I want you, Charlie and me to be a family. Is it the idea of Fauré that stops you speaking?' he demanded roughly. 'You deserve better than some other woman's left-overs!' he ground out passionately. 'Give me the chance and I'll make you happy, Rachel—happier than he ever could!'

Benedict loved her; he was prepared to stay in England and live a life that stifled him. Getting her head around these fantastic revelations required more mental agility than her punch drunk-brain was capable of.

'You can't love me. I'm...'

'The woman who haunts my dreams,' he said fiercely. His arms closed so tightly around her, she could hardly breathe. The compelling message in his eyes distracted her from such mundane necessities. Who needed to breathe when the man you loved looked at you with such fierce, possessive tenderness?

'The woman I want to live with, grow old with—the woman I want to love if she'll let me. Will you?' he growled throatily. She could feel the tension stretching the muscles of his lean body.

She raised a trembling hand to his face. Her fingers trailed with wondering tenderness down his lean cheek before coming to rest against his lips.

'But you didn't come near me after...'

'After you threw me out of your bed—your life? You're

surprised?' he asked, one dark brow lifting ironically. 'I had this idea you might find you missed me more than you thought. Being the optimist, I thought you might be more malleable after a dose of deprivation. I don't know what it did to you, but I've been half out of my mind.'

'I thought you and Sabrina—'

'Despite appearances, I have explained to Sabrina in words of two syllables or less that I'm not interested in resurrecting a very tepid on-off thing we had last year.'

She nodded, accepting his words without reservation.

'I tried to think about the future, tell myself you were just passing through,' she recalled huskily. 'But when I was with you I couldn't protect myself at all. Nobody has ever made me quite so miserable.' Her eyes glowed with a deep warmth as she raised them fully to his. 'Or quite so blissfully happy.' She watched the anguish drain from his face to be replaced by a sensual satisfaction. 'I fell in love with you, Ben, even though I knew there was no future.

'You have to understand that it's a long time since I did anything without considering the consequences. With you I knew what the consequences would be and I did it anyway! If I hadn't been so concerned that Charlie was falling in love too in her own way, bless her, I'd have spent every waking second I could with you before you went away. It wasn't pride or common sense that made me pull back—just a desire to protect her. We come as a package deal.'

'I always did have my father's eye for a good deal. I've got a ready-made family. Besides, Charlie picked me out personally,' he reminded her, resting his forehead against hers and placing his big hands firmly over her rounded bottom. 'She brought me home—home to you.'

'Ben!' What followed was half sob, half husky laugh; translated, it meant rapture and it was lost in the warmth of his mouth. For several breathless minutes there were no words at all.

'Someone might come back in,' she mumbled as his lips nuzzled hungrily at her neck.

'Yes,' he agreed without much interest.

'They'll…they'll…' She twisted her throat to enable him to complete his self-appointed task of kissing every inch of her throat.

'They'll be jealous,' he suggested helpfully.

'You need a shave,' she grumbled, rubbing her chin against his jaw. 'It reminds me of…'

He lifted his head and the devilish glint completed the disreputable image. 'Who does it remind you of?'

'You know perfectly well who,' she said ruefully. 'I felt sorry for you,' she added with a sniff.

'And the rest,' he scoffed. 'Your interest wasn't any more pure and elevated than mine was; admit it.'

'You're so conceited, Benedict Arden.'

'At least you're not dishonest enough to deny that reform wasn't the only thing you had on your mind,' he teased.

'Just as well, because as it turned out you're beyond redemption.' Her expression suddenly sobered. There was something she had to tell him. 'Talking about honesty…'

'Do I sense a confession coming on? Should I sit down?'

'Maybe.'

Her gravity was contagious; Benedict looked cautiously down at her.

'About Christophe.'

She felt his hands, which had rested lightly on her shoulders, tighten. 'I know he's Charlie's father but—'

'No, he's not.'

'Pardon?'

She hurried on. 'He's not Charlie's father. He's her uncle; his brother Raoul was her father.'

'Raoul Fauré.' He frowned, trying to place the name. 'The racing driver?' He rubbed his forehead; there was a dazed expression on his face.

'Yes,' she nodded. 'I met him when I was working for Christophe and his wife as an au pair. I think he was bored one weekend; that's all it amounted to for him,' she admitted. The only thing it hurt to admit that now was her pride. 'I was dazzled by the glamour and you know the rest.' It was amazing that the whole sorry incident could be summed up in two sentences. 'The accident happened not long after.

'Christophe and Annabel never knew; not until Christophe spotted the same family resemblance you did.'

'My God, Rachel, I wanted to kill the man,' he grated hoarsely. 'I thought he was trying to worm his way back into your life, and worse still I thought you wanted him to. I suspected he might even pull some stunt like getting custody of Charlie.' He groaned. 'You have no idea what it's been doing to me imagining...' His dark eyes were filled with pain. 'Why did you let me think that, Rachel?'

'Charlie didn't have a proper family because I was a silly, gullible girl who only saw what she wanted to. I didn't want to do that to her again. She's so fond of you and she kept dropping hints the size of bowling balls about us... I thought you were leaving.' Her eyes pleaded for understanding.

'Like Raoul left you,' he said grimly.

'There's no comparison,' she denied swiftly. 'I've never loved anyone before you.' Lovingly she took his face between her hands and spoke from the heart. 'I didn't have the experience to be able to distinguish infatuation from the real thing back then. I do now. *Nothing*,' she said fervently, 'is more real than the way I feel about you. I needed the excuse to drive you away because I didn't have the backbone to do it by myself.'

'Does Charlie know about her father now?'

'Yes.' She searched his face anxiously for a clue to what he was thinking. What effect had her confession had?

'Everything?'

'Well, I didn't say, Your father wouldn't have remembered my name a week after you were conceived.'

'I can see you wouldn't want to do that. Has he reached heroic proportions yet?'

'You don't mind?' She gave a relieved sigh.

'Mind! I mind all right. But sometimes the truth comes at too high a cost. Charlie needs to be protected from the un-varnished version of this particular truth.'

'I was afraid you'd...'

'I love Charlie,' he said quietly. 'Of course I care about what that bastard did to you! I'd like to climb onto the pro-verbial old white charger and right all the wrongs that have been done to you if I could. That's what you've done to me, woman.' He shook her gently. 'And if you tell anyone I ad-mitted that I'll never forgive you.'

'My lips are sealed...'

'To every other man but me,' he agreed complacently. The expression on his face as his glance dwelt on the passion-swollen pink outline made her tremble.

'When I think of what you must have gone through. This time it'll be different,' he vowed.

'You want a baby?' She knew she was smiling in a dopey, foolish way, but he didn't seem to mind.

'Don't you?'

Rachel gazed up at the big man she loved. 'Yes, please.'

'Let Charlie's dad be a dashing hero; I can live with it. If you love me I can live with just about anything!'

'I think she's more interested in her real-life hero.'

'And who might that be?'

'He's already spoken for,' she whispered, emotion throb-bing in her voice.

'Then you'll marry me?'

'Yes!'

The couple twisted around at the sound of the jubilant cry.

'Nat said you were getting married. She was right!' Charlie was dancing around the room.

'I'm always right,' came the modest reply. 'So where is the bubbly?'

Benedict looked down at his startled bride-to-be, a smile in his eyes. 'Well, you have to say yes now.'

'I thought I did.'

'I might need to hear you say it more than once.'

The idea that Benedict, big, strong, confident Benedict, could need reassurance brought an emotional lump to her throat.

'Can I have a horse? Just a small one. Ben's got loads of money; Nat says so. Nat says—'

'Nat says too much.'

'Excuse my avaricious offspring.'

'She brought me home to you; I'll forgive her anything,' he said with extravagant good humour.

Rachel sighed. He still had a lot to learn. 'That statement will come back to haunt you,' she predicted.

'We've laid to rest the only phantoms that had me worried.'

Rachel returned the pressure of his fingers and nodded mutely back. 'I should have known you were trouble the first moment I set eyes on you,' she teased huskily.

'Forget first impressions.' He dismissed them with a shrug. 'It's lasting impressions that count. Did I make a lasting impression on you, my love?'

'The eternal variety,' she confirmed happily.

EPILOGUE

RACHEL tucked the light sheet over the chubby limbs of the sleeping baby.

'Is he off?'

Rachel leant back into the strong arms that encircled her. 'At last,' she confirmed. 'Turn on the baby alarm, will you, Ben? It went well, didn't it?' she said happily as he returned to her side.

He looked down proudly into his wife's face and nodded. She'd worked incredibly hard organising the christening of their first son and she'd still managed to look good enough to eat all day—and all day he'd been wanting to do just that.

'Isn't it about time you put your feet up? The others are on the veranda knocking back the left-over bubbly. That baby's had enough toasts today to last him clear through till his eighteenth birthday.' He smiled at the small figure of his sleeping son.

'I'll just…'

'No way,' he said, hooking his arm around her trim waist. 'I've already looked in on Charlie and she's flat out.'

'Is it time to worry when you start answering my questions before I've asked them?' she asked, giving one last peek at the sleeping baby before closing the door quietly behind them. Things were good with Charlie right now. She'd got her pony. They were just gritting their collective teeth and waiting for the dreaded teenage hormones which were almost upon them.

'Don't worry, you can still surprise me. Last night for instance…' He let out a soundless whistle.

'Shh!' she said warningly. She reached up and pressed her finger to his lips. 'Someone might be listening.'

He nibbled the finger before saying reflectively, 'That didn't seem to bother you last night.'

'Ben!' she remonstrated, trying to sound angry, but the grin kept peeping out.

She smiled a lot these days. Life wasn't one long party by any means. Ben worked long hours. She could understand his fascination with this land now, and shared it to some degree. Her real passion was reserved for this man who was as complex and demanding as this wild country. Getting to know both better was a rewarding, deeply fulfilling experience. Seeing how much he loved it here made her appreciate how great a sacrifice it would have been for him to stay in London—a sacrifice he'd been prepared to make for her!

They strolled in companionable silence outside to the veranda. The warm night air was soft on her bare arms. Rachel glanced upwards; she didn't think she'd ever take this marvellous night sky for granted.

'So Ruth knew as soon as she heard the name that Rachel was the girl,' they heard Tom Arden say. He was wiping tears of laughter from his face.

'So did most of the legal fraternity in the city,' his wife's soft voice explained.

'So you went to school with this woman who was actually in there when he...?' Natalie asked, her eyes sparkling.

'Did you hear William?' Benedict asked his wife softly. 'I'm sure I...'

'No.' He looked extremely uncomfortable when she waved aside his interruption and leaned forward, her hands on the wooden white-painted rail. With a half smile on her lips she strained her ears to catch the punchline of a story that seemed to be amusing their guests. Between the Ardens and the

Faurés, who had also come over for the christening, they had a full house.

'Yes, I went to school with Carol.'

'Can you imagine Ben of all people rushing into the ladies' after a woman?' Natalie gave a crow of laughter. 'I'd have loved to see his face when the door opened and it wasn't Rachel.'

Rachel turned to her husband. 'You did that?' Her voice alerted their guests for the first time to their presence.

'I thought you were in there. If you laugh, so help me I'll…'

'I wouldn't do that,' she gasped. It was too much; her lips began to quiver and then her face crumpled. 'I wish I'd been there.'

'Me too,' he said with feeling.

The expression on his face made her break down all over again. 'S-sorry,' she hiccuped.

'He threatened to knock down the door,' Tom added.

'Don't,' Rachel pleaded, 'it hurts.' She clutched her aching stomach muscles.

'So does being a figure of fun,' her husband assured her.

'If we're talking pain I'll have you know I lost a tenner to Ruth betting you weren't about to get married. How was I to know she had insider information?' he asked the assembled company in a disgruntled tone.

Sir Stuart Arden got to his feet carefully; he'd spent most of the day appreciating Australian wine. 'To Rachel and Benedict. I always said she was the girl for him, didn't I, Emily?' He looked to his wife for support and she rolled her eyes heavenwards.

'I'll second that,' Ben said, taking Rachel very firmly by the shoulders. 'And if you can stop laughing at me for a second I'll give my own toast—to your lovely lips.'

'Just a second?' she taunted just before he swooped. He made her eat her words in the nicest possible way.

**He's a man of cool sophistication.
He's got pride, power and wealth.
He's a ruthless businessman, an expert lover—
and he's one hundred percent committed
to staying single.**

Until now. Because suddenly he's responsible
for a BABY!

HIS BABY

An exciting miniseries from Harlequin Presents®
**He's sexy, he's successful...
and now he's facing up to fatherhood!**

On sale February 2001:
RAFAEL'S LOVE-CHILD
by Kate Walker, Harlequin Presents® #2160

On sale May 2001:
MORGAN'S SECRET SON
by Sara Wood, Harlequin Presents® #2180

And look out for more later in the year!

Available wherever Harlequin books are sold.

Visit us at www.eHarlequin.com   HPBABY

#1 *New York Times* bestselling author

NORA ROBERTS

brings you more of the loyal and loving,
tempestuous and tantalizing Stanislaski family.

Coming in February 2001

The Stanislaski Sisters
Natasha and Rachel

Though raised in the Old World traditions of their
family, fiery Natasha Stanislaski and cool, classy
Rachel Stanislaski are ready for a *new* world of love....

*And also available in February 2001 from
Silhouette Special Edition, the newest book in the
heartwarming Stanislaski saga*

CONSIDERING KATE

Natasha and Spencer Kimball's daughter Kate turns her
back on old dreams and returns to her hometown, where
she finds the *man* of her dreams.

Available at your favorite retail outlet.

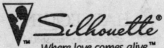

Where love comes alive™

In March 2001,

presents the next book in

DIANA PALMER's

enthralling *Soldiers of Fortune* trilogy:

THE WINTER SOLDIER

Cy Parks had a reputation around Jacobsville for his taciturn and solitary ways. But spirited Lisa Monroe wasn't put off by the mesmerizing mercenary, and drove him to distraction with her sweetly tantalizing kisses. Though he'd never admit it, Cy was getting mighty possessive of the enchanting woman who needed the type of safeguarding only he could provide. But who would protect the beguiling beauty from *him...*?

Soldiers of Fortune...prisoners of love.

If you enjoyed what you just read,
then we've got an offer you can't resist!

Take 2 bestselling love stories FREE!

Plus get a FREE surprise gift!

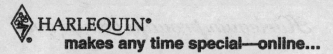